"Several un[...] [...]
us at rapid s[...]

Tech swung [...] the [...] Escarpment [...] shallow term[...] [...] Valkyries. Whoever the pilots were, they were flying a motley assortment of craft, with parts begged, borrowed, or stolen. In a glance, Tech spied grotesque fabrications of wheels and wings, bubble canopies and drive turrets, flags and banners, signs and sigils, radomes adorned with the toothy snarls of predators or whiskered with weapons.

Outlaws!

Occupying the open cockpit of one craft was a big, yapping dog wearing flight goggles and a long black scarf.

"Cyrus, I don't have any weapons!"

"Then it's best to avoid them."

"I'm with you."

Tech and Cyrus swerved northeast for the safety of the Ribbon, but the cyberoutlaws anticipated their course and intercepted them before they had gone a Network mile. Disabling code chased Tech's unresponsive craft, forcing it south, back toward the abyss, perhaps in the hope that he would ditch.

"Cyrus, I need some velocity soft!" Tech said. "The Dino's no match for these guys . . ."

*Also by James Luceno:*

WEB WARRIORS: Memories End

# WEB WARRIORS

# DIMENSION X

# JAMES LUCENO

BALLANTINE BOOKS • NEW YORK

A Del Rey® Book
Published by The Ballantine Publishing Group
Copyright © 2002 by Red Sky, Inc.

www.delreydigital.com

ISBN 0-345-44472-8

Manufactured in the United States of America

First Edition: November 2002

OPM 10 9 8 7 6 5 4 3 2 1

# WEB WARRIORS

# DIMENSION X

WEB WARRIORS

The contrived sky of the Virtual Network had been gouged by the swift transit of an unidentified intruder. The rend ran straight as a jet's contrail, but yellow as the peel of a sunripened banana. At moments the intruder was a dazzling sphere outfitted with radar dishes that might have been giant ears, and at other moments a silver-hulled spacecraft, blunt nose aglow and rear thrusters blazing, sporting a pair of longlashed cartoon eyes.

The transformation from one to the other was neither a trick of the virtual light nor evidence of sloppy programming, for clearly the intruder was intent on sowing confusion. Why else would it have announced itself with such a bold calling card and affected such obvious disguises? Like all the craft and constructs and highways that made

up the Network, the intruder was only an amal-
gam of complex codes, but that didn't mean it
wasn't capable of wreaking havoc.

Faced with the possibility of cyberterror-
ism, Network Security was quick to respond,
launching tight formations of pursuit programs
modeled after buzzsaw blades. Spinning ener-
getically, the saw-toothed disks gushed foun-
tains of disabling code that lit the false sky like
metal filings flung from a grinding wheel. But
the intruder merely held to its course, knocking
cybercraft violently aside or deleting them entirely as it plummeted like a meteor, deeper into
the Network.

NetSec upped the ante.

From shield emplacements tucked into the
elaborate crowns of the Mitsuni Spire and the
IBM NeoDome—the Network's tallest constructs—came powerful salvos of defensive fire.
Lime-green hyphens of corruption poured upward, striking the intruder repeatedly, and tearing loose segments of programming that trailed
behind the dual-natured ship like colorful
streamers.

The whirling pursuit programs converged,
adding bursts of minimizing code to an already
furious light show. Forced to grow more calcu-
lated in its movements, the intruder began to
perform more like a piloted craft than a free-
falling rocket. Narrowing its cartoon peepers, it
executed abrupt swoops and dog-fight rollovers
that left the security buzzsaws foundering in its
wake. Then it veered sharply, hurtling toward

the cityscaped heart of the Network with the unbridled enthusiasm of a child racing for a playground.

By then it had attracted the attention of a dozen or so daring cyberjocks flying custom craft, all of whom were attempting to plot the intruder's course and match its speed. The pair of fliers at the head of the pack were all but nipping at the intruder's tail.

"It's heading straight for the Ribbon!" the male pilot slightly in the lead told his wingmate over their dedicated audio link.

"Wild!" she said. "I've never seen such a speed junky!"

Their user names were Tech and Isis, and they were piloting the hottest craft in the pack. Tech's was a modified, bubble-canopied AirSpeeder 6000, bristling with infoscanners, uplink arrays, grappling hooks, and harpoon launchers. Isis' was a serpent-prowed skiff, replete with contoured wings and billowing sails, that would have been right at home in some fantasy writer's version of ancient Egypt. She called it "The Prowler." Bulging aftermarket turbodrives were allowing both craft to keep pace with the intruder, although their repeated attempts to actually come alongside the thing had failed time and again.

"I'm getting all kinds of chatter from the fliers at Ziggy's," Isis said.

"Shut it down. This is our case."

"Can we catch it?"

"Hello! I thought I heard someone question

the skills of the Vega brothers. What do you say to that, Dr. Marz?"

"Take some MaxBlast 4.7 and call me in the morning."

Tech's younger brother, Marz, was navigating for both fliers from the office of Data Discoveries, a cybersleuth agency devoted to tracking missing or misplaced data. It was Marz who had customized the craft, and it was thanks to his ingenuity with software that Tech and Isis were managing to mirror the intruder's maneuvers.

"We need a solid kick in the butt, bro," Tech said. "What else you got running besides MaxBlast?"

Programs scrolled down a window in Tech's visor: Turbo 7.5, Speedfreak, Mondo Gonzo . . .

"Here's something I haven't tested yet," Marz said, "an upgrade of Ripper."

"Beautiful," Tech said.

He could almost picture the sly grin on his brother's face. If there had been even a moment to spare he might have peeked out from under his data visor to throw Marz a knowing wink.

"Hit me."

Marz sniggered. "Hang onto your headgear."

Tech and Isis did just that as the bootleg software loaded. Then, instantly, their separate craft streaked forward, with g-force acceleration their motion-capture vests let them feel deep in their chests. Aware of its pursuers the intruder dove, but to no avail. Soon Tech and Isis were flying side by side slightly above the ship, whose big, round eyes tracked them with exaggerated apprehension.

Isis ramped up her craft's code descrambler. "I'm getting audio."

Tech isolated the intruder in a readout window in his data visor and magnified the image. Using his joystick, he realigned one of the Air-Speeder's side-looking scanners and boosted the audio gain to his earphones. What he heard made him sit up straighter in the old dentist's chair that served as his flight seat in the real world.

"Sounds like it's laughing," he said.

"Cackling's more like it," Isis said a moment later.

Tech listened more closely. "I swear, I know that laugh from somewhere . . . Marz, is this thing piloted or glitched?"

"No one knows," his brother said, "or at least CiscoSoft's not saying."

"CiscoSoft?" Isis said. "They produce entertainment soft, don't they?"

"TV shows, movies, Netcasts . . . you name it," Marz said. "Cisco sent out the SOS to Felix, but if we don't hurry, every flier in town is going to be in on this."

Data Discoveries' owner and head cybersleuth Felix McTurk was ever on the alert for jobs that could catapult the agency to the big leagues.

"I just wanna nail the thing," Tech said.

Chasing the intruder had been thrilling enough

to allow him to forget, even temporarily, his lingering concerns about Harwood Strange—comatose as a result of having helped unravel the mystery of Cyrus, the artificial intelligence who had partnered with Data Discoveries only two weeks earlier—and about the dire warning Tech had received from unknown parties on the completion of Cyrus' reassembly.

A warning he had yet to share with anyone else, including Cyrus.

"Maybe this rogue has something to say," Tech suggested. "Is Grappler running?" Grappler was a data link that wouldn't harm the rogue program.

"Locked and loaded," Marz said.

Returned to big-eared meteorite mode, the intruder had flattened the angle of its descent and was closing on the Network's principal thoroughfare, the Ribbon. But instead of making straight for CyberSquare, at the head of the Ribbon, the intruder had turned east to avoid the heavy traffic around Grand Adventure, the Network's premier race course construct. Tech, by contrast, knew those traffic patterns by heart, and so simply pitched the AirSpeeder 6000 into the thick of the snarl, weaving the craft from lane to lane and from level to level, and in the end managing to gain a few precious seconds on his fire-tailed quarry.

By the time Grand Adventure's entry gates were looming in the near distance, Tech had the intruder centered in the visor's targeting reticle.

While the fingers of his right hand tapped positioning code into the joystick's bat-wing control pad, his left hand enabled the AirSpeeder's grappler function.

Flooring the interface rig's accelerator pedal, he fired a triple-pronged data-hook.

It was a clean, precise shot, aimed for the rim of the largest of the craters that pitted the intruder's dorsal surface. But who- or whatever was responsible for defending the intruder hadn't been caught napping. In the blink of an eye the intruder transformed from rough-surfaced sphere to gleaming spaceship. Shrugged off by the now seamless craft, the grappler flailed ineffectually in the false wind.

"Guess it doesn't like attachments," Isis said, coming alongside Tech.

"It's smarter than we are," Marz muttered in the melodramatic voice of a mad doctor from a 1950s SF movie. "Only science can conquer it."

"Science or a harpoon," Tech was quick to counter. "That'll take some of the flight out of it."

"Just what Captain Ahab said before Moby Dick bit off his leg," Isis said.

"Huh?"

"Skip it. I keep forgetting you only read comic books."

"And proud of it."

"Harpoon's up and running," Marz broke in. "Target one of the thruster ports."

Unlike Grappler, which allowed a flier to attach

him- or herself to a program, Harpoon carried a compressed packet of crippling code that could stop a program dead in its tracks.

Tech called on Ripper for added velocity, then threw the AirSpeeder into a power dive. Falling in behind the intruder, he opened Harpoon and launched a barbed quill straight into the intruder's right thruster.

The intruder went wide-eyed and yelped angrily. Issuing what sounded like cartoonish backfires, it streaked away.

"Heads up!" Isis said.

Tech instantly saw the reason why. Perturbed by Tech's sting, the intruder doubled back and tried to ram him off course. Tech climbed out of reach. He was on the verge of firing a second harpoon when the intruder commenced a steep corkscrewing descent for the cluster of buildings that surrounded CyberSquare.

The first construct to feel the intruder's wrath was Atomic Music. Punctured, the construct loosed a storm of musical notes and stanzas, all of which began to waft down toward the wooded park. The intruder joined the shower of icons, activating short-lived sound bites as it powered past the dislodged musical signatures, ultimately fashioning them into a familiar theme song.

"Hey, I know that tune!" Tech said, as the intruder tore into the labyrinth of paths that wound through CyberSquare.

Tech followed, careening through an obstacle course of suddenly airborne fliers, many of whom were bounding above the treetops as if pinched in the rear by surprise. At the far end of the square, the intruder was nosing upward toward the inclined face of InfoWorld, dropping bulbous data-bombs from bays that opened in its belly.

Below, cartoon stars and chirping birds were pinwheeling around dozens of bomb-struck cybercraft. Eruptions of short-lived balloon onomatopoeia accompanied the bombs: *Boom! Bamm! Thwack!* . . .

Tech laughed in astonishment. "Hey, how'd it do that?"

"Target's changing course," Marz updated. "Headed back for the Ribbon, all speed."

Tech and Isis veered for the highway, launching harpoons without success. Rolling its eyes at them, the intruder touched down on the Ribbon with a nerve-jangling screech. Thrusters flaring out, it barreled on, gradually assuming the polished roundness of a bowling ball, and flattening countless vehicles under its heft.

Tech could feel for the flattened fliers. Almost every visitor to the Network had experienced a hard delete or suffered through the brainaches that were the consequence of being thrown off-Network. But it was pain of a whole different caliber to learn that not only had you "tossed your bytes," as fliers said, but also that the craft you'd spent long hours assembling or purchased at great expense had lost all its attached enhancements and been reduced to a basic vehicle. It was like entering the Net at the controls of a

Maserati and suddenly finding yourself peddling a tricycle.

The now squinting spheroid intruder was barreling south at a good clip, fast approaching the fairy-tale castle of Peerless Engineering, where Network Security had erected a massive firewall. Multi-barreled batteries resembling surface-to-air missile launchers began to range in. But the intruder was not to be outsmarted. Well short of the anti-intrusion moat that surrounded the castle, it bounced off the Ribbon and disappeared into the warren of Network sites that lined the Peerless Underpass.

"Gutter ball!" Tech shouted, as he and Isis accelerated to keep up.

"Enable ScatterShot!" she shouted back.

Weapons concealed in the AirSpeeder's bow and the skiff's serpent head peppered the intruder with prolonged bursts of minimizing code and little by little the retreating bowling ball began to lose mass. But at the same time it was gathering speed. With security gates snapping closed behind it like overwrought pinball machine flippers, the intruder rampaged on, slamming into site after site, and igniting each like struck bumpers.

Isis hooted. "Who programmed this thing—Marty Morph?"

"That's it!" Tech said. "That's who this is! I *knew* I recognized that laugh and theme song!"

"But Marty Morph's a cartoon character."

"A CiscoSoft Entertainment cartoon character," Marz chimed in.

"And he's loose in the Network," Tech said.

"Surprised you didn't recognize him right away," Isis said, "seeing how cartoons are your thing."

"Ha," Tech said flatly.

"Seriously, how could Marty M get loose?"

"All the more reason to catch him and find out," Marz said.

"So, what's the problem?" Isis said. "Isn't this what you guys are supposed to be good at?"

"We're on it, Isis," Marz said harshly.

Tech and Isis continued to trigger fusillades of disabling code. Assailed from all sides, Marty Morph—spinning like an Englished cue ball and loosing the modulating, contagious laugh that had earned him legions of fans—pulled yet another trick from his bottomless bag. Self-compressed to an even more compact orb of chaotic energy, *the morphing maniac of Mainstream* flew up the tailpipe of a double-decker tourist bus, standing the zebra-striped thing on its rear wheels, then propelling it forward, whooshing great puffs of steam from cone-topped whistles it sprouted on each side.

Passengers began to bail out, springing in panic from the windows and making graceless exits to the real world. Again, Tech winced. The out-of-control vehicle had to be sending scores of cybersystems into overload, rushing fliers from site to site without design, like the advertising loops that could sometimes ensnare hapless Net-surfers.

No sooner had the archaic bus emptied than it

became a bug-eyed, big-wheeled monster truck, emitting blasts of noxious exhaust as it trundled over every obstacle in its path. Swerving to avoid another roadblock, it clambered into Sony Plaza and started to scale the inclined face of Sony's pyramid-shaped construct.

"Throttle back," Tech warned. "He's going to jump!"

Isis banked acutely in the nick of time.

Marty, the topsy-turvy pickup truck, wheelied and leaped, sailing straight through the transparent roof of Create-a-Creature. In seconds, a menagerie of exotic cyberbeasts was stampeding out into the Network. Tech and Isis zigzagged their craft through packs of two-headed giraffes, troops of goat-monkeys, flocks of crow-men, prides of lion-beetles.

Last to exit the ruptured construct, and plainly eager to separate itself from the pack, scurried a nearsighted rabbit, tugging a pocket watch from its vest and muttering, "I'm late, I'm late."

"Get that wacky wabbit!" Tech and Isis said in unison.

Marty Morph saw them coming and hopped. Rebounding from the Ribbon as if it were a trampoline, he vaulted the security firewall at the base of the Peerless mountain and soared straight between the castle's tallest turrets, as if they were goalposts.

Tech and Isis decelerated, as much to avoid being knocked off-Network by the castle's code-corrupting weaponry as to keep from venturing any closer to Peerless Engineering than was necessary. Two weeks earlier Tech had gone up against Peerless, and he had no desire to engage the powerful corporation a second time. Marty, however, showed no fear. Deftly evading the worst of Peerless' flaming-arrow barrages, he shot over the top of the castle and vanished from sight.

"He went over the edge of the Escarpment!" Tech said, astonished.

A kind of digital divide, the Escarpment, and the abyss below, separated the commercialized Network from the relatively unpopulated and unpoliced fringe—the Wilds—which had long been the domain of hackers, renegades, and cyberoutlaws.

"Fool toon fell into the abyss," Isis said.

"He could be headed for the Wilds along the rim highway," Marz said. "Tech, you can cut him off by jumping."

"Go for it," Isis encouraged. "I'll see if I can spot him, in case he's riding the rim."

"Harwood's flight plan is loading," Marz said.

Tech studied the data display windows in his visor. "Flight plan received."

"Good luck, Tech," Isis said.

"See you in the Wilds."

Tech shoved the joystick to one side, sending the AirSpeeder into a lengthy come-about. The Peerless Castle expanded in front of him, sinister beneath its fanciful mix of towers, turrets, and keeps. Careful to steer clear of Peerless' well-defended cyberspace, Tech stuck to the Ribbon, which looped around the castle, at the very frontier of the commercial Network.

Soon he was behind Peerless, directly above the spot from which he had made his one and only leap from the Escarpment. Theoretically, anyone in possession of Harwood Strange's flight plan could undertake the leap. But it took more than a complex sequence of codes to guarantee success. For that you needed the right craft and ability to control that craft with utmost precision. It was like going up against the Master Ghoul in a blood-lust adventure game: cheat codes could lead you to him, but after that it was all about skill and timing.

Tech's solitary jump had been his only means of outfoxing a deadly foe that had chased him from Peerless' hidden domain. A cyber-entity of unknown origin, that foe—Scaum—had been charged with preventing the resurrection of Cyrus, the AI. But Scaum's best efforts had been thwarted, and where Cyrus lived again, Scaum, with any luck, lay moldering at the bottom of the abyss.

Tech continued to swoop down toward the cliff.

It had been his assumption since separating from Isis that Marty Morph was already headed west along the Escarpment rim, bound for the Wilds by the only tried-and-true route. But assumptions were just that; and, in fact, the rogue cartoon character who had assumed the identity of a Wonderland rabbit was instead crouched on the Ribbon, in the shadow of the castle, shifting his gaze between his outsize pocket watch and the gaping virtual fracture in front of him.

Tech chortled to himself.

Wearied by all the disabling code Tech, Isis, and NetSec's long-range batteries had poured into him, Marty was probably too weak to embark on even the long route to the Wilds, let alone risk bridging the abyss with a leap of faith. One carefully placed harpoon, and Marty could simply be hauled back to CiscoSoft Entertainment.

More assumptions.

The AirSpeeder had no sooner begun to angle down when the spectacle-wearing white rabbit lifted its head, and all the innocence and animation drained from its face like light at the end of the day.

The long ears flattened and became twisting, bifurcating horns. The oval cartoon eyes became ruby-red slits. The outsize front teeth became fangs, tipped with drops of viscous venom. And the body lost its soft furred limbs and elongated, coiling in the shadows like some monstrosity loosed from horror movie hell, raising a triangular head into the air to meet Tech halfway.

It was all Tech could do to arrest his descent, much less escape by jumping the abyss.

Fear—irrational but irrepressible—flooded into him.

The hulk drew itself up, lolling its fat tongue hungrily as it fixed its baleful gaze on the Air-Speeder. It unhinged the lower jaw of its fearsome head, as if preparing to ingest the hovering craft whole.

But instead it spoke, sibilantly and succinctly.

*"You were cautioned about interfering in our business—Tech."*

WEB WARRIORS

Unlike the sanitized eye-candy of the Network, with its glittering towers and pearlescent domes, its spires and structures borrowed from every historical era and architectural style, the Wilds was an undulating plateau of dense forests, craggy mountains, and enchanted lakes—a cyberized land of Magic, designed in tribute to an Earth long gone, where imagination reigned, and myths and legends flourished. In place of the corporate constructs of the grid were floating cities and underwater domains, sand-dune deserts, gloomy caves, and quirky hovels. Where bright highways like the Ribbon bisected the Network grid, the Wilds had meandering paths lit by magic lanterns or guttering torches, under an indigo dome of twinkling stars. But for all the allure, it was also a lawless realm of empty, hazily coded stretches, and hidden traps—the cyber-equivalent of quicksand pits and white-water whirlpools. Worse, the Wilds was home to roving bands of pirates and outlaw hackers, capable of overwhelming the craft of lone fliers, and using those craft as a means of raiding home or office cybersystems for sensitive information.

The most recent addition to the Wilds was, in fact, the large, eight-sided construct Cyrus had built to house himself during his reassembly, and had since become the Network headquarters of Data Discoveries—much to the worry of many a wary hacker.

The Data Discoveries octagon lay to the south of the route Isis had taken from the Escarpment, where, at its western terminus, it dwindled to the size of a shallow ledge. Off to her right, she could just make out the Data Discoveries sign that topped the octagon, but she saw no sign of Marty Morph. She could understand how she might have beaten the berserker toon to the Wilds, but Tech should have been waiting for her at the edge of the abyss, opposite the Peerless Castle.

Wondering what had become of him, Isis was maneuvering The Prowler closer to the rim of the Escarpment when something whizzed past her. The craft's proximity and the speed of its passing sent her out of control and whirling out over the edge. The Prowler's wing-shaped stabilizers failed, the sails sagged, and the void yawned beneath her like the gaping mouth of a gargantuan beast.

The fate of those who challenged the abyss, either by dint of misadventure or reckless daring, was rarely in doubt. While a handful of lucky fliers had managed to deploy emergency chutes and ride data currents back to the grid, the rest had been jerked back to the real world in the harshest fashion, resulting in cases of chronic vertigo, blindness, even temporary schizophrenia. The only method for avoiding a hard delete was to execute a graceless exit, though even that carried its own risks to mind and body.

In the Data Discoveries flight room, Isis lifted her hands from her joystick and raised them to her interface headset.

*Better a migraine headache than a fling with cyberdaze,* she told herself as she prepared to rip the headset away. But just then something grabbed The Prowler by its uplifted stern, swung it back over the Escarpment, and maneuvered it to the relative safety of the Wilds.

"Nice save, Tech," Isis said when she could. "I was sure I was dirtbound."

"Always a pleasure," her rescuer answered in a somewhat childish voice. "Though I'd appreciate proper credit."

Isis found herself accompanied by a black-eyed, button-nosed program gremlin, bright blue from its pointed ears to its splayed feet.

"Cyrus!" she said in happy surprise.

While equipped with more than enough crunching power to portray himself as just about anything he chose, or to navigate the Network in the flashiest of cybercraft, Cyrus continued to affect the guise of the mischievous program gremlin that had originally come to Tech's rescue, in much the same way the artificial intelligence had just come to Isis'. But the bright-blue wrapping was as much guise as disguise. With program gremlins commonplace in the Network, Cyrus was free to move about without fear of attracting the attention of those who wished him ill or worse, including his alleged designer and "father," Skander Bulkroad, president and CEO of Peerless Engineering.

Despite his successful reassembly, the AI was still somewhat impaired, with gaps in his memory regarding the motive for his murder ten years earlier. But even in the two weeks he had been with Data Discoveries, he had helped solve a couple of well-paying cases.

"Sorry I was delayed," Cyrus said. "I was finishing up a file search for Felix when he assigned me to the CiscoSoft case. Looks like Marty Morph has escaped into the Network."

"So it is him," Isis said.

"CiscoSoft character mod-star package. It launched from CiscoSoft's NetTV site."

"Can't be good for business when your star toon goes on a cyber-binge."

"Not to mention that CiscoSoft will be held accountable for all the damages Marty Morph inflicts."

"I still don't understand how a toon could go rogue."

"CiscoSoft recently installed a neural net computer to supervise NetTV programming," Cyrus said. "Marty Morph may have been launched by mistake."

"Innocent or not, we've got a job to do." Isis paused to scan the virtual surroundings. "Where the heck is Tech?" She opened an audio link to Marz. "Are you there?"

"Right where you left me."

"What's with your brother? Why isn't he here?"

"He's headed your way now—entering the Wilds twenty klicks cyber-north-northwest."

Isis reoriented her compass and targeting soft, and gazed across the abyss in the direction of the Peerless Castle, but still saw no sign of Tech. "He should have been waiting for me. What happened?"

"Chill, Isis. Tech started his jump, then stopped."

"Why?"

"I don't know. Ask him yourself."

Just then Tech's AirSpeeder shot into view, following the same route Isis had taken.

"Why didn't you jump?" Isis said immediately. "I thought you were going to head Marty off at the pass."

"Glitch in the flight plan," Tech said. "I'll explain later. Which way did Marty go?"

Tech sounded agitated, but Isis couldn't tell if he was exasperated, angry, or frightened. Before she could ask, he opened a channel to Marz.

"The AirSpeeder isn't cutting it, bro. I need an upgrade."

"Opening the garage," Marz said. "Thrasher'd be good for the Wilds."

"I already know what I want—the V-7 Blackout."

"No go, Tech. It's not Net-tested."

"So? I feel a need for speed."

Windows opened in Tech's and Isis' data visors, revealing row after row of cybercraft Marz had designed and built. A fighter jet with a downsloping radome, the Blackout V-7 sat in the trial bay. Isis upgraded The Prowler for another of her own creations, a razor-toothed Venus Flytrap she called Deceiver. Cyrus, as ever, was content to remain a program gremlin.

"I've picked up Marty Morph's trail," the AI reported.

The three resumed the pursuit, relying on Marz to navigate them deep into the Wilds, where the far-from-home toon—back to being a big-eyed Flash Gordon rocketship—was circling around, looking for some mischief to perform. Catching sight of the Blackout, the Deceiver, and the bright-blue gremlin, Marty's eyes crossed in alarm, and—with comical sounds of a speedy departure and a cloud of dust—he shot for a remote area of the Wilds, beyond which the Virtual Network had yet to be written.

"Think like a cartoon star," Isis suggested to Cyrus, as they picked up Marty's trail.

The largely uncharted western boundary of the

Wilds was defined by a mist-shrouded range of desolate mountains, known, against all appearances, as the Uplift. There Tech and Isis found Marty Morph in desperate search of an exit. Marty had grown three additional pairs of eyes, and all of them were darting about, to dizzying effect. The toon's anxiety increased when he realized that Tech and Isis were positioning their cybercraft along the only route back to the Escarpment and the Network grid beyond.

Cyrus, meanwhile, had found what he had been searching for: a twisting canyon that penetrated a short distance into the Uplift before meeting a sheer wall. At the mouth of the canyon, Cyrus had painted a cartoonish "exit arrow," before disappearing inside. Whizzing on the scene, Marty Morph's eight eyes fell bulging on the arrow and he screeched to a halt; then rocketed off into the canyon.

Tech and Isis chased him, arriving just in time to hear a loud *splat* reverberate from the canyon's walls. Inside, they found the renegade toon flattened against a false tunnel entrance Cyrus had coded into the precipitous wall.

"Gets 'em every time," Isis said.

Now a shiny disk held fast to the wall, Marty Morph blinked his eyes in bewilderment, then began a slow slide to the floor of the canyon. Hitting bottom, the toon tried once more to morph into an enlivened spacecraft, but the disk did little more than sputter and fume, and at long last collapsed tails up like a spun coin.

Unexpectedly, however—and with a protracted growl—something black as a moonless night began to seep from the disk.

"Look out!" Tech warned, just as he and Isis were closing in.

The black program gathered itself into a ball of fury and raced so powerfully past Tech's and Isis' craft that they had to call on Cyrus' help to keep from being slammed into the canyon walls.

"What was *that*?" Isis asked.

Trembling in memory of the cyber-monstrosity he had faced at the castle only moments earlier, Tech said nothing. But Cyrus offered an opinion.

"That," the AI said, "was whatever infected Marty Morph's program to begin with. A huge cache of convoluted code, obviously hidden in the neural net computer."

"A virus?"

"No, not a virus."

"Well, whatever it was, I got a data signature," Marz announced, "and a course heading."

Isis maneuvered the Deceiver to face Tech's Blackout, then indicated the groggy disk at the base of the canyon wall. In the frequently imitated voice of Marty M, the disk was mumbling, "Anybody get the license plate number of that truck?"

"Game over, except for reeling it in."

But the Blackout didn't move.

"What's with you? Don't you want to bring him in?"

"You should have the honor," Tech said.

Isis laughed. "Trying to earn the maiden's hand, is that the idea?"

"Whatever. He's all yours."

"If you say so. Where do you want me to dump him, Marz?"

"At the octagon. I'll forward him from there—with best regards from Data Discoveries."

Isis dropped the Deceiver to the floor of the canyon. Opening the Venus Flytrap's jaws, she took careful hold of an unusually docile Marty Morph. When she ascended, the toon was trapped inside the jaws like an unlucky insect.

Tech watched, waiting for something horrible to leap from the captured program. When nothing happened, he followed at a cautious distance.

## Chapter 3

In the real-world headquarters of Data Discoveries—a couple of cramped rooms, high in Manhattan's Empire State Building—Tech and Isis, still snugged into their separate flight seats, took themselves through a set of routines intended to return them to normal awareness with a minimum of side effects. The routines were in a very real way analogous to the decompression ascents a deep-water diver is obliged to make before surfacing, if he or she hopes to avoid a case of the bends.

Casual or infrequent visitors to the Network needed only to take off their headsets, let go their joysticks, and log off. For deep-immersion fliers, however, the transition was more complicated, owing to the intensity of the visual and auditory impulses the interface gear allowed them to experience—especially when used in conjunction with the X-treme, and typically untested software programs Tech and Marz were continually trying out. Reemergence required that they sit through a series of diminishing optical images while their visors gradually went from Network-active to transparent mode. Then, and only then, was it safe for them to remove their headsets, slip out of their motion-capture vests, and return to normal reality. Though often compared to waking from a dream, the passage from virtual to real was in fact closer to waking from a sleepwalker's dream—a dream so real as to be indistinguishable from waking life.

The headaches and personality disorders that ensued from hard deletes and graceless exits were the result of short-circuiting those routines.

Since the body was tricked even more easily than the mind, it was not unusual for a cyberjock to awaken fatigued, or even exhausted, as if after rigorous exercise, and so Isis let out a loud yawn as she removed her simple headset and electrode-studded motion-capture vest.

She was a tall and freckled fifteen-year-old, with ice-blue eyes and mounds of flaming red hair. She came from money—her father and uncle were renowned designers of cybersystems—but she dressed street, in bold and often tight-fitting clothes.

Isis glanced at her reflection in a hand mirror and groaned.

"Cyberface," she muttered. She tugged at her

baggy eyes and tried corralling some of her obstinate curls into a purple scrunchy.

Her flight seat—a padded, deep-blue recliner with built-in control pedals—had come free with the office's most recent acquisition, a water-cooled SV3003 cybersystem, at which Marz sat—limpid-eyed, dark-complected, small for his fifteen years—surrounded by high-def and 3-D monitors, time-saver keyboards, and the bright, stainless-steel arc of the console itself, which was sometimes compared to the instrument panel of a jumbo jet.

In the office's second flight seat—a dentist's chair, retained as a souvenir of the office's former occupants—Tech came to, stationary for several seconds, and wearing a worried look, as if he hadn't transitioned well. Sixteen and fair-haired, he played down his handsome features by never shaving, and wore whatever clothes did the greatest injustice to his lanky frame.

Marz brought each of the fliers Whammy chocolate bars and cans of Impact Cola, then raised his own soda in a toast. "To another successful retrieval by Data Discoveries. Case solved."

"Felix is going to flip," Isis said. "CiscoSoft is a major player."

Marz frowned at her, then looked at Tech. "S'up, bro? No joy in Smallville?"

Tech stared blankly at him.

"How come you're not toasting?"

Tech gazed at the can of soda in his hand as if

he had only just become aware of it. "Oh, sure," he said finally, lifting the can to his mouth and taking a short sip.

Marz and Isis traded quizzical looks.

"Spill it," Isis said.

Tech remained distracted. "What?"

"For starters, why you didn't jump the abyss."

Tech averted her gaze and made a nonchalant motion with his right hand.

Isis narrowed her eyes. "Been there, done that?"

"He's easily bored, you know," Marz said, affecting an upper-crust British accent.

"You're already a Network legend, so why bother, even where there's good reason to jump?" Isis shifted her gaze to Marz. "He told me the flight plan was glitched."

Marz's thick brows met in a V. "It was?"

Tech opened his mouth to say something, then reconsidered and started again. "Throttle back—both of you. The flight plan's fine. It was only me that was glitched."

Isis let her sudden concern show.

"I was thinking that it might be too soon for another jump," Tech said, after a second false start. "Because of what happened last time."

"The Netquake," Marz said.

Isis looked from Marz to Tech. "You really think your jump caused the quake?"

"Look at it this way," Tech said. "Harwood Strange and his hacker apprentices wrote the abyss into the Network to prevent Peerless Engineering from expanding into the Wilds. So when someone—namely, me—finally bridged the abyss . . ."

"The jump rattled the base codes of the entire Network," Marz said.

"I don't want to be responsible for another quake. Not after all the damage the last one did."

Isis bit her lower lip. "That kinda makes sense."

Tech turned to his brother. "Any ideas about what flew out of Marty M after he hit the wall?"

Marz shook his head. "Nope, but I got a signature. I thought I had a course heading, too. But I lost track of the thing right after it recrossed the abyss."

Tech stared at him in puzzlement.

"It was just too fast." Marz fell silent for a moment, then brightened. "I'll analyze the data fragments. What matters is that CiscoSoft Entertainment has its toon back, and, thanks to us, the Network has been saved from who knows what craziness."

Isis joined him in smiling. "What should we ask Felix for—another flight chair, new software?"

"How 'bout an early end to school," Marz suggested.

"Oh, shit!" Isis said. "I'm late for class!"

"That makes three of us," Tech said, already running for the door.

Felix McTurk's smile was so radiant it could be seen through the thick panels of tinted glass that darkened the lobby of the Empire State Building.

"By that grin, I'd say that things must be going swell, Mr. McTurk," the uniformed guard behind the security counter said as Felix approached.

Felix ran his identity card through a swiper. "We solved a case that's really going to put Data Discoveries on the map."

The head honchos at CiscoSoft Entertainment had assured Felix of that when he had met with them the previous day. Well, practically assured him. But no matter. Capturing Marty Morph would be different than having solved the mystery of the disappearance of Cyrus Bulkroad— only *the* most baffling mystery of the past decade. Felix had been forced to keep quiet about Cyrus, as much for the sake of the AI as for Data Discoveries, since Peerless Engineering would make for one dangerous foe. But once word got out about Marty Morph, clients would be lining up at the door, eager to hire Felix McTurk—and associates. He shook his head in wonder. Less than a month earlier his whole world had been on the verge of collapse. Then Cyrus had come along and everything had changed. He still didn't trust the AI completely, but, unlike Tech and Marz, Cyrus carried out whatever assignments Felix gave him, and without complaints.

Felix rode an express elevator to the sixty-fifth floor. In the marble corridor, well-heeled lawyers and attractive young secretaries passed by him without a word of greeting. Things would be different soon enough. He stood proudly for a long moment in front of Data Discoveries' glass-paneled door, then entered.

"Can I help you?" a youthful female voice uttered.

Felix gazed across the small waiting room at the gum-chewing, blue-haired teenager seated behind a newly installed desk. Silver encircled her thin wrists and cuffed her ears. She was dressed in black from head to toe, and her lips were painted a glistening maroon.

"What?" he said, recognizing her as one of Tech and Marz's friends from the Safehaven Group Home.

"Please have a seat, and Mr. McTurk will be with you in a minute."

"Aqua, it's me—Felix."

Aqua Brockton smiled, then blew a big pink bubble and popped it. "Totally."

"Then it's okay for me to go to my office?"

She nodded. "Go right in."

Felix shook his head, took off his baseball cap and glanced around at the empty waiting room. "Looks like your first day on the job's going to be a breeze."

"Oh, but you already have a client," Aqua was quick to reply. "Tech and Marz are talking—uh, interviewing her now."

"Tech and Marz are," Felix said. "Why do I even bother coming to work?"

Aqua blew an even larger bubble and popped it. "Totally."

Felix stepped into the office suite's flight room where the Romano Twins—Norse and Farlin, two more of Safehaven's orphans who also had installed themselves at Data Discoveries—were filing hardcopy. When neither of the dark-haired, twelve-year-old twins acknowledged him, Felix felt his newfound happiness begin to ebb.

Maybe it would be easier just to relocate Data Discoveries in the group home, he thought—dismissing, for the moment, what head councilor Fidelia Temper might think of the idea. That way he could employ *all* the kids.

He peeked through his office door before opening it completely. Tech and Marz were talking with a plainly dressed woman of fifty or so. The woman's face was lined with worry, and her hands were clasped tightly in her lap. Tech had his sneakered feet up on Felix's desk, and Marz was scribbling notes. Isis—the only Data Discoveries employee who had an actual home life—wasn't present.

"Don't let me interrupt," Felix said, opening the door fully.

"Felix!" the boys said in unison.

Tech swung his feet off the desk and sat up straight in Felix's swivel chair. "Uh, Mrs. Squabbish, this is Felix, er, Mr. McTurk. Felix, Mrs. Squabbish."

Felix walked to the desk and shook the woman's hand.

"Hello," she said. "Your partners have been very polite in listening to me."

"My partners," Felix said, skewering them with a glance. "I'm sure they have."

"Mrs. Squabbish was just explaining about her husband," Marz said.

Felix smiled at her. "Start at the beginning, Mrs. Squabbish."

She took a deep breath. "My husband, Ken, has been a frequent flier since the earliest days of the Virtual Network. He's been a good husband and a devoted father, but every moment he hasn't spent with us has been spent surfing the Network. Even at work, his job allows him to spend time visiting sites and wherever else it is you people go."

"I take it, then, that you're not a cyberflier," Felix said, shooing Tech from his chair and sitting down.

"Heaven forbid. The real world is excitement enough for me. In any event, starting about two weeks ago, I began to notice a change in Ken. He was spending more and more of his time in the Network, and even in the few moments he spent with us he didn't seem to be, well, *himself*." She paused to compose herself. "I realize how that must sound, Mr. McTurk. But we've been married for twenty-five years, and I know Ken like a holobook. He just isn't himself any more. Physically he's the same. But emotionally, he's . . . he's like a robot!"

Mrs. Squabbish's anxiety was palpable.

"Cyberspace can have a peculiar effect on people," Felix said, trying to sound soothing. "It's not uncommon for some fliers to lose themselves completely, especially if there's a wish to escape—"

"You don't understand," she interrupted. "Ken had no reason to seek an escape. Everything was perfect at home, and at work. He told me he'd discovered some sort of new area in the Network—a domain, he called it. And whatever was there, was so . . . compelling, that he kept returning. That's when he really began to change."

At Mrs. Squabbish's mention of a new domain Felix glanced at Tech, since Tech, too, had found his way into a new domain two weeks earlier. But Tech returned a subtle shake of his head, as if to say that the two domains couldn't possibly be the same.

"For Ken to neglect us for the Network," Mrs. Squabbish was saying, "this place, this domain—Area X, Ken said—must be very powerful."

Tech and Marz's eyes lit up. "Cool," they said in unison.

Mrs. Squabbish took a stuttering breath. "I think the domain did something to him, Mr. McTurk. I think it stole part of his mind!"

Felix didn't respond immediately. Cybersleuth agencies like Data Discoveries often appealed to an odd assortment of clientele. The waiting room was frequently filled with slovenly dressed loners sporting cryptic tattoos and cyber-interface glasses, and carrying file folders stuffed with pages of coded jottings, or suspect software disks they hoped to sell to Marz.

Had Mrs. Squabbish arrived on a more typical day, she might have thought she had wandered into a hackers' convention rather than a home for teenage runaways. As a result, Felix had grown accustomed to dealing with prospective clients who were certain that their computer systems had been overwhelmed by viruses born in outer space; cyberjocks who claimed to have been spirited involuntarily to unknown realms in the Network; wives and/or husbands who had become convinced that their frequent-flier spouses no longer seemed themselves, and had become a new order of "missing persons."

"I'm sorry, Mrs. Squabbish," he said finally, "but this sort of thing is out of our league. We track down missing data, disappeared information, and misplaced property."

"But I thought, since this has to do with the Network and all . . ."

Felix shook his head in sympathy. "I suggest you take this matter up with a physician or a psychologist."

"You think I'm crazy, is that it?"

"I didn't say that. I'm simply saying that we can't help you."

Mrs. Squabbish nodded and stood, then walked stiffly to the door. But before exiting she turned to Felix. "You're wrong, Mr. McTurk.

Ken's illness has something to do with the Network. I'm certain of it."

Felix waited until Mrs. Squabbish was out of earshot, then said, "Were you listening in, Cyrus?"

"I was," the AI said through a set of carefully concealed speakers.

"Good job on the CiscoSoft case, by the way."

"Thank you," Cyrus said. "But Tech, Marz, and Isis deserve equal credit."

Felix narrowed his eyes at the brothers. "Oh?"

Tech swallowed and found his voice. "We, uh, might need a note for missing algebra."

Felix started to reply, then exhaled in aggravation, and swung back to the mirrored wall. "Any thoughts on what Mrs. Squabbish had to say?"

"Some."

Felix depressed a button on the desktop and the mirrored wall parted, revealing a hidden room, partitioned by plate glass, containing a dozen seven-foot-tall data storage towers, the sum of which housed Cyrus' terabytes of code. The octagon in the Wilds the AI had constructed for himself had been supported by a score of different servers Cyrus had managed to infiltrate during his reassembly. But since then, and with Cyrus' help, Felix had been able to lease the data storage towers, into which Cyrus had gradually—and very covertly—relocated himself.

The AI communicated with everyone by means of cameras and microphones, and a large flatscreen that displayed him as a big-eyed, blue-skinned program gremlin.

"So when is a person himself and not himself?" Felix said toward one of the audio pickups. "How does somebody become a 'robot'? "

"Apparently when one stumbles into Area X," Cyrus said. "I'm well aware of the conflicting rumors about the place, but considering what Tech and Harwood experienced inside the Peerless Castle, I think you were wrong to refuse the case."

Tech was nodding his head in agreement.

"We could have at least interviewed the husband, or helped them find a doctor."

Felix shook his head. "We've got a business to run, Tech. And in this business you have to learn to distinguish between the ordinary fringe and the lunatic fringe." He swiveled his chair to the office's mirrored wall. "I need a logical explanation, Cyrus, not Network mumbo jumbo."

Cyrus came onscreen. "All right. Then it's possible that it isn't the woman's husband who has changed, but the woman herself. There's a certain brain syndrome that can account for her delusion. When a particular portion of the brain becomes injured, it is frequently the case that, while a person recognizes another, he or she fails to experience any *emotional* attachment to the person, and so becomes convinced that the person cannot possibly be his or her husband, wife, father, mother, etcetera."

Felix smiled smugly.

"Yeah, well, it would have to be a virus to

account for the numbers of cases we've heard about and turned away," Tech said to Cyrus.

"It could very well be a virus," Cyrus replied, "since the condition is usually temporary, and the patient heals without treatment."

"That doesn't mean someone couldn't become possessed by a Network program."

"Yeah, like in an old horror movie," Marz said soberly. "*Attack of the Body Thieves. Demons from the Red Planet.*"

"Felix asked for a logical explanation," Cyrus said. "Accordingly, I'm stating that I don't know of any cases of certified cybernetic possession."

"And Area X is part of Mrs. Squabbish's delusion, too?" Tech said.

"Perhaps—since she can't account for the sudden change in her husband's personality in any other way."

"But suppose, just suppose," Tech continued, "that Ken Squabbish really did discover a new domain."

"Excepting for the moment the hidden domain you infiltrated, rumors have long circulated of mysterious places concealed in the far corners of the Network."

"This is like, what, person 1507 that's found Area X?" Marz said.

"Area X is nothing more than a legend," Felix said.

Tech swung to him. "Yeah, but what happens when the legends turn out to be true?"

"Name one that has," Felix said.

Marz glanced at Tech and answered for him.

"The legend of the cyberjock who leaped from the Escarpment and lived to tell about it."

Felix nodded pensively while the brothers were smiling, then said: "Then there's the one about the *two* cyberjocks who repeated ninth grade for fifteen years in a row."

**WEB WARRIORS**

"Oh, the horror! Oh, the humanity," Marz said with counterfeit dread, as he and Tech were heading north on Lexington Avenue, bound for Safehaven Group Home. "To have to walk instead of fly. To have your field of view limited to 180 degrees. Not to be able to write portals where you want or need them . . ."

He gestured broadly to the tall buildings that rose to all sides, to the security cameras affixed to every other storefront and street sign, to the ubiquitous police officers and armed guards. "Where's the magic?"

"You seem to be the only one having a problem with it," Tech said.

Marz glanced up at him. "You don't?"

Tech shrugged. "Sometimes the real world can feel like an escape."

"The opposite of what Mrs. Squabbish's husband thought, is that what you mean?"

"I guess."

They turned west on 54th Street and approached the entrance to the former hotel that now housed Safehaven. Marz stood in front of the security camera and hit the intercom icon on the system's touch screen.

The pinch-featured face of Fidelia Temper studied them from the display monitor. "You're ten minutes late for room check."

"An alien ate my dog," Marz said.

Fidelia scowled. "Make sure you read the chore list. No weekend privileges unless all chores are completed by noon tomorrow."

"Home sweet home," Tech said when Fidelia's image had disappeared from the screen.

Marz swung to him. "Man, sometimes I really wish we were on our own."

Tech clapped him on the back. "Bro, we've always been on our own."

Two additional security doors stood between them and Safehaven's lobby. They carded themselves through both doors, and were aimed for the hallway that led to their room when they heard a commotion emanating from the communal lounge. Hurrying inside the lounge, they saw Furio Cane, Safehaven's most successful bully, victimizing one of the home's youngest residents, a tow-headed nine-year-old everyone called Go-Bop.

"Gimme the game," Go-Bop was shouting, leaping to try to snatch a game disk from Furio's extended hands. "It's my turn!"

"It's your turn when I say so," Furio said, dangling the disk just out of Go-Bop's reach.

Dressed in black jeans and a black sleeveless top, he had long muscular arms and an arcane symbol shaved into his cropped hair. Where Tech and Marz's parents had died in a plane crash, word had it that Furio's parents had deliberately abandoned him. He and Tech had had numerous run-ins, usually as a result of Furio's picking on Marz.

"Furio, give him the game," Tech said from across the room.

Furio stiffened, turned slowly around, and grinned. "Beat it, Vega. Go hide in the Net for a few years."

"Just give him the game, man," Tech said sullenly.

"Or what—you're going to email me a nasty note?"

Tech was about to reply when Furio's snarky grin became a glare and his thick forefinger punched the air. "Stay out of my business, dumbass."

Tech's face flushed with anger. For a moment he was transported back to the Peerless Castle, where almost those very same words had been hurled at him the previous morning. Before he could stop himself, he rushed Furio.

Furio planted his right foot behind him and raised his fists. Ducking under Furio's powerful right cross, Tech grabbed the larger boy around the waist and sent him backward into the wall.

The collision shook the wall with enough force to send a dozen DVDs cascading from a shelf onto Go-Bop's head.

Three of Go-Bop's peers turned from the TV long enough to leap to their feet, shouting, "Fight, fight!"

Furio hammered Tech on the back with his elbows, until Tech dropped to his knees. But Tech caught Furio's ankles as Furio was sidestepping and brought him down. Furio's chin met the thinly carpeted floor with a loud *crack!*, and Tech fell on him with a vengeance, raining punches on the back of Furio's head. Furio squirmed and managed to roll over, launching a left hand that caught Tech square in the nose. Tech's head snapped back, but he continued to land punches, now on Furio's face and upper body.

Rooted in place, stunned by the unexpected ferocity of his brother's attack, Marz heard hurried and telltale footsteps in the corridor and quickly threw himself between the two combatants. Sustaining hits from both, he had barely managed to separate them when Fidelia Temper burst into the room. Fists balled and nose bloodied, Tech was standing over Furio, whose chin was split and whose right eye was already beginning to swell shut.

"Stop it!" Fidelia roared. "Stop this immediately!"

She advanced, grabbed Tech by the wrist, and whirled him away from Furio. Then she glowered at Furio until he relaxed his fists and backed off. Planting her hands on her hips, she stared everyone down.

"Who started this?" she demanded.

"I did," Tech, Furio, Marz, and even Go-Bop replied in unison.

Fidelia's nostrils flared and her eyes became slits. "I'll ask one more time: Who did this?"

"He did," everyone said.

"Fine. Have it your way," Fidelia said. She pointed to the hallway. "All of you—to your rooms. You're barred from using the lounge until I say so."

The younger kids moaned. Tech and Marz winced.

Furio's departing glance at Tech promised revenge; Go-Bop's was one of hero worship.

Tech and Marz hadn't left the room when Fidelia added, "And don't for one moment think I'm unaware of Aqua's new job. Just who does that data detective think he is, trying to use Safehaven as some temp agency? You're not a group of Oliver Twists he can simply recruit to further his own dubious ambitions. You can tell him for me that I intend to notify child services."

"Felix isn't breaking any laws," Marz said.

"Not yet, he isn't, Marshall."

Marz and Tech didn't speak until they reached their room. Tech's nose was still bleeding, though not badly. Marz grabbed a couple of ice cubes from a small fridge.

"Here."

"Leave me alone," Tech said, without looking at him.

Marz frowned. "You really waled on Furio, bro. You okay?"

Without a word, Tech grabbed the ice, walked straight for his laptop cybersystem, and slipped into his headset.

Tech's personal deck was nowhere near as powerful as the office cybersystem; so only a few of Marz's custom vehicles were stored in memory, and all of them ran slowly. Worse, the software packages that gave Tech a heads-up on Network Security wouldn't run at all. But what the deck did have was a library containing more than a thousand of Tech's favorite songs, a bashing cache of which he loaded before logging on.

Happily distanced from the latest catastrophe at Safehaven, and with Inner Rage's synthbeat pulsating in his eardrums, Tech sliced his boomerang-shaped glider down the Ribbon, weaving the craft in and out of traffic, almost baiting security to chase him. Approaching the Peerless Castle, he navigated into the Ribbon's outermost lane, which looped counterclockwise around the construct, then ascended one level to place himself just above the tallest of the castle's grove of crenellated turrets and flag-bearing spires.

On orders from Felix, Tech hadn't tried to re-infiltrate Peerless, even though some of Cyrus' missing memory bytes were still nested inside the castle—including memories that might explain how the dark cyber-entity Scaum had come into being, and why Skander Bulkroad had decided to have Cyrus, once his personal AI, terminated.

Tech circumnavigated the castle, eventually bringing the glider to rest directly over the spot where the black presence that had infected Marty Morph had revealed itself, reiterating the warning Tech had received to cease having anything to do with Cyrus.

Or had the white rabbit really transformed into a serpentine beast?

Perhaps the transformation had been Tech's delusion, conjured by his fear that Scaum, too, had reassembled, and was lying in wait, eager to exact revenge on Tech for having been outwitted at the abyss.

In the hope of preventing just such an encounter, Tech had altered his Network identity a dozen times, and yet he continued to feel watched and stalked by unseen enemies, sometimes as much in the real world as in the Network. Just flying this close to Peerless was enough to bathe him in sweat beneath the motion-capture vest. That was why he had "waled" on Furio, as Marz had put it. Furio's words had been the final straw.

But how could he confess any of his fears to Marz, Isis, Felix, or Cyrus, when he still hadn't told them about the original warning he had received? He certainly had been meaning to tell them. But each time, the words never made it past the tip of his tongue, in part out of dread that Felix would ban him from entering the Network at all, if he learned that Tech had been targeted by someone—or *thing*.

Once upon a time the Network had been Tech's unfailing deliverance from the defeats and disappointments of real life. Now the two realms might as well have been identical. Save for the presence of Marz and Felix, of course—Tech's family. He feared for Marz's safety as much as he feared for his own. If Harwood Strange could be left comatose, Tech told himself, what horrible fate might befall Marz simply for being Tech's brother? Scaum had already showed him a vision of that.

And now Isis was in the mix. Intelligent and attractive, she was more than he could ever wish for in a girlfriend—and still a long way from being one—but at least there was a chance for that. Much to Marz's occasional dismay that she had become a member of the team so quickly—despite the hardware she had brought to Data Discoveries—Tech was forever encouraging her to join in their Network jaunts. But didn't he owe it to her to confess that flying with Cyrus was potentially dangerous—even if Isis should decide to exit his life as swiftly as she'd entered it?

Tech realized that he was grinding his teeth.

The anger he thought he had left behind in his Safehaven bedroom had caught up with him.

Leaning into the joystick, he sent the boomerang-shaped glider angling toward the Escarpment and to the very edge of the abyss.

*"Show yourself if you're down there,"* he screamed at Scaum in his thoughts. *"Let's have it out here and now!"*

No one answered him.

Beneath him there was only the swirling gray mist of yet-to-be-written code—of nothingness.

He hovered above the rim and gazed across the digital divide, hectoring himself to jump. Despite what he told Marz and Isis, he didn't believe that a jump would really cause a second Netquake, and he didn't care if it did. His deck should be able to handle the flight plan that had been Harwood Strange's gift. He just needed to launch himself and get it over with.

He moved closer to the edge.

Just jump, he told himself. *Jump!*

But in the end, seeing in his mind's eye Scaum's taloned hand reaching up to snare him, he couldn't bring himself to make the leap.

Despair welled up inside him.

Why did he and Marz have to be the ones who got the copy of the software bundle Cyrus had doctored to ensure his resurrection? What had either of them ever done to deserve an even worse life than they had had B.C.—Before Cyrus?

He didn't know what to think, what to believe, what to do.

His thoughts pinwheeled like the night sky. He shouldn't have to sort out everything by himself, he thought. Someone needed to come along and tell him what to do next.

It was then that motion caught his eye and he

saw Cyrus appear alongside him at the edge of the Escarpment, that silly gremlin likeness so at odds with the profound mind Tech had come to know over the past few weeks.

"If you're looking for Scaum," the AI said, "I already checked, and he's nowhere to be found."

"That's not what I want to hear. I want you to tell me that Scaum's dead, or deleted, or whatever happens to cyber-fiends like him."

"That isn't the case, Tech. I know instinctively that, like me, Scaum has the ability to reassemble himself."

"Great."

Tech wondered what Furio and some of the others at Safehaven might make of his having become fast friends with an artificial intelligence—much to *Felix*'s occasional dismay. At times, Tech attributed his bond with Cyrus to the fateful encounter inside the Environmental Protection Agency, or the fact that Tech had actually been *inside* Cyrus' octagon. But he understood that the reasons went much deeper than that, and had little to do with Cyrus' not being a younger brother, a close friend, or a father figure.

What informed the friendship was a shared sense of mystery about the past. In Cyrus' case, that mystery was explicit—portions of his memory were missing. But with Tech the mystery rose from a *feeling* that he, too, was incomplete. Perhaps all orphans felt that way, to some degree, he told himself. But where Marz seemed to have found his calling in designing stunning cybercraft, and his place at Ziggy's Cyberchop Shop, Tech had yet to discover his place in the scheme of things. More—though he would never admit it to anyone—Tech sensed that, like Cyrus, he had a destiny to fulfill. And that was what ultimately bound them: personal mysteries that had turned them into fellow explorers, seekers after the truth, and poet warriors along the way.

"I suspect that whatever possessed the Marty Morph program was related to Scaum," Cyrus said.

Tech blew out his breath. "Yeah. One moment it was a screwball cartoon rabbit, and the next it was a snake-headed demon hissing a warning at me."

"Why didn't you say something sooner, Tech?"

"Because for all I know I imagined the whole thing."

"You didn't," Cyrus said a long moment later. "The Marty Morph program was much more dangerous than Marz, Isis, and Felix believe it to have been. More than simply glitched, it was possessed by something of tangible power."

"People who aren't themselves, programs that aren't themselves . . . What's going on, Cyrus?"

"Maybe I'd have an answer for you if I could remember my entire past—beyond remembering that my own father wanted me dead because of something I did, or some secret I learned."

Tech could detect actual *pain* in Cyrus' words. He was more than simply an AI. "Cyrus, you're not the only one Peerless is after," he revealed at last.

The gremlin's big, innocent black eyes fixed on him.

"Remember when you invited all of us into the Network to see the Data Discoveries sign you'd erected over the octagon?"

"Yes."

"When we were returning, just before I exited the Network, someone spoke to me, warning me not to have anything more to do with you, and threatening that I could end up like Harwood if I didn't obey."

"Peerless Engineering," Cyrus said. "My father . . ."

"I don't know who else could it be," Tech said softly.

Cyrus moaned, dejectedly and resonantly. "Even with Scaum in pieces, the darkness persists."

Marz sat silently on the edge of his bed, arms folded across his narrow chest. Tech was only eight feet away but, lost in cyberspace, he might as well have been in another world. Marz could stand only a minute of it before he donned his own headset, chose a craft from his laptop's garage, and piloted himself into the Network.

Sights and sounds shifted and intensified, but his concern for his brother remained unchanged. He wanted desperately to strike at the heart of whatever had undermined Tech's spirits, and to restore the normal order of things, where Tech was usually the one worried about Marz.

Not wanting to attract attention, Marz was flying an innocuous-looking blue-metalflake '63 Chevy Impala. Wide-bodied and low-riding, with a curvacious tail end and plenty of chrome, the craft was meticulously modeled after one of the first pleasure craft to have navigated the then newly founded Network, more than a decade ago. His destination was Ziggy's Cyberchop Shop, a hot spot on the north Ribbon, and a gathering place for cyberjocks and silicon monkeys who enjoyed swapping the latest bootleg soft and sharing information about craft and cyber-engine design. Ziggy's was often the site of racing challenges, and sometimes the starting point for the races themselves.

You could hear the place long before you could see it, though Ziggy's neonlike sign towered over just everything else along that stretch of the Ribbon, including its closest neighbor, Dinky's Cyber–Take-Out. Music of all modes and tempos blaring. Engines revving, purring, humming, whistling, throbbing—whatever sounds the pilots wanted you to hear when you clicked on them for an audio signal. Craft peeling out, pulling wheelies, or rocketing off to run time-trial laps around the Mitsuni Spire or the IBM NeoDome. Ships of unending variety arriving or leaving: show craft, racing craft, chopped and channeled buses, wafer thin saucers, quad-finned missiles. Two-tone, three-tone, ten-tone,

veined in fiber optics, cut like gemstones . . .
Performance governed only by the rules written
into the Network itself.

*The rules*—friction and gravity being the worst
offenders.

What craft might fly the virtual skies if not for
those rules!

It was an ongoing and often heated debate,
since many fliers believed that, for all its squeaky
clean orderliness, the Network was too close a
reflection of the real world. The thinking of the
original planners—many a Peerless Engineering
technopath among them—was that by mirroring
*reality,* they were making the Network more accessible to mainstream fliers, in their sturdy family SUVs and cookie-cutter podcraft.

For the mainstream, the Network cityscape,
with its faux skyscrapers and Las Vegas–style
show palaces, was entertainment aplenty. But
anyone who had grown up with the Network
understood—as had most of the jocks who
haunted Ziggy's—that cyberspace had the po-
tential to be a *separate* reality, where the enve-
lope could be pushed to the max. Unfortunately,
those same idealists lacked the money, power,
influence, and wherewithal to realize their visions, and so had to content themselves with
Peerless Engineering's notion of cyberspace, as a
kind of fantasy land of commerce and politically
correct distraction.

Ziggy's though—considering that it managed
to combine elements of an Indy 500 mechanics

pit, a drive-in hamburger joint, and a space station—represented a step in the right direction.

On arriving you would see hundreds of craft parked side by side, displaying stats and sometimes the user names of the pilots, surrounded by groups of cyberjocks in their own craft, marveling over curvilinear cyberframes, engine cowlings, mirror finishes, pilot nacelles, opalescent canopies, turbochargers, friction compensators, traction boosters, and velocity stacks. If you knew code—if you *really* knew code—you could see how the designers had achieved their results. But that did nothing to lessen the admiration. And if you weren't keen on writing code, Ziggy's was where you could meet people who, for money or barter, could make your dreams come true.

And that's what Ziggy's was really about: talking soft, creating soft, swapping soft ... sampling, synthesizing, sequencing, experimenting—all with an eye toward becoming a trendsetter, the one whose designs everyone else emulated, even if for only a week. It was more about art than design, and the fact that everyone borrowed from or one-upped everyone else was what kept things fresh and vital.

Here, Marz was a legend.

Here, it made no difference that, in the real world, he was short and a spazz at shooting hoops.

Drifting about in search of something interesting, he spied a cluster of fliers gathered around a vehicle that resembled a mating of arachnid and Hummer. Marz checked his lens display to see if the Hummer's owner was displaying his user name, and was surprised to learn that it was Ramlock. One of a handful of people Marz knew in both the real and cyber worlds, Ramlock—Travis, in the land of the living—was a tall, model-handsome, athletic twenty-year-old who had graduated from the same Manhattan high school Marz and Tech attended—occasionally, at any rate. Along with being a flash on the football field, Travis was also a wizard with code, and had designed and built some of the most dynamic craft the Network had ever seen. A year back, Ramlock and Marz had struck up a friendship after meeting and swapping soft at Ziggy's, where a lot of tight friendships were forged.

Marz waited for a relatively quiet moment in the chatting to insert a hello, then flashed his detection code, in case Ramlock failed to identify him in the classic Chevy.

"Hey, Marz!" Travis said over an audio link. "Cherry craft! What're you hiding under the hood?"

"Aah, only an F/X 450 MicroLam, with a Series Three overdrive and a Covelly phase booster."

"Bitchin'! That thing must tear! Hey, I hear you and your bro are flyin' from an SV3003."

"With Graviton vests," he said.

"That's top of the line 'ware, dude! Where'd you guys come by it?"

Marz's ongoing ambivalence toward Isis prevented him from copping to the full truth, so instead he said, "We've got our connections." Then, to change the subject, he added: "Nice data lock on that Hummer, Ramlock. You planning on doing some off-line in the Uplift?"

"You like her, huh? She's for the show—for *Cyberchallenge*. I've been picked as a contestant."

Marz thought for a moment. "New virtual reality program, right? A bunch of jocks compete to survive in different cyber-environments, or something."

"That's most of it. Premieres live, the day after tomorrow."

"*Cyberchallenge?*" someone said. "I figured the Hummer for Ramlock's attempt at marketing the first Netquake-proof craft."

"I was online when that quake went down," another flier said. "Crashed my system, deleted my best craft, and had me seeing spots for a week."

"Half the fliers that were lurking at Peerless that day had the same thing happen," a third voice added. "I even heard that some of them *disappeared,* like, for real."

"Yeah, right," a female voice said. "Another cyber legend is born."

"I heard that Peerless *caused* the quake. They were experimenting with detonating code—"

"—to prepare for expanding the Network into the Wilds," a dozen separate voices finished.

"Dude, that one's weeks old."

"No way the hackers in the Wilds would allow that," someone added. "That's why they wrote the abyss, in the first place."

"Yeah, but I heard that somebody jumped it," another said.

Marz was tempted to brag about Tech's recent feat when the whistling revving of a powerful engine drew everyone's attention to Ziggy's entrance. Announced by a series of explosive reverberations, a craft whirled onto the scene, the likes of which had never been seen at Ziggy's or anywhere else on the Ribbon. *Craft*, actually, since the thing was constantly changing shape, like a time-lapse photographed cloud going from sailing ship to elephant to anvil, each transformation punctuated by flares of unworldly color and symphonic chord progressions. With clutch-popping screeches, it leaped from place to place, phasing in and out of view; here one moment, there the next, as if running time trials for a race through the fourth dimension.

Every 'jock present checked his or her visor readouts to see if the shapeshifter was displaying an identity. And when the craft's pilot responded to the requests, everyone abandoned Ramlock for the newcomer.

Bios7 was himself—or herself, since no one knew his actual identity—a Network legend, oft-touted as being the best pilot on the grid. He flew the fastest ships and his technique was impeccable. He had challenged Tech to a race around the Peerless Castle. Tech had been so eager to prove himself that he had taken the loop too fast and had shot over the edge of the Escarpment. The last-second deployment of a safety chute—by Marz—was the only thing that had saved Tech from a hard delete.

When he wasn't racing, Bios7 was known to fly some outrageous craft—all of which had been designed by others—but the one he was piloting now didn't bear the signature of any of the top designers Marz was familiar with.

The ship was something new and incredible.

A score of 'jocks were already assailing Bios7 with questions by the time Marz succeeded in maneuvering the Impala close enough to have a good look at the shapeshifter. When someone asked Bios7 if he had obtained the software designs through The Hackers Outlet—a well-known franchise—Bios7 ridiculed the idea that Tsunami or any of the other Boruans who owned the outlet could supply soft of the caliber needed to create what he was flying.

"Then where did you get it?" someone asked.

Bios7 laughed. "Let's just say that there are areas of the Network you fangeeks don't even know about."

"Come on, man, don't go evasive on us," someone said at last. "Where'd you score the soft-ponents?"

"It wouldn't matter if I did tell you," Bios7 said, "since entry's by invitation only."

Marz aimed his scanners at the still changing craft. The code he retrieved was impossible to read. It scrolled down a display window in his

visor like an alien language. He was studying it
intently when someone hailed him over a private audio frequency.

"Hey, Marz, what do you think of my craft?"

Marz recognized Bios7's voice, and nudged
the Impala around to face the shapeshifter head-
on.

"What kind of flash trash is that?"

"Jealous already, Marz."

"Well, what soft is that?"

"Uh, uh, amigo. That's classified." Bios7
paused, then said, "Where's your brother? I've
been looking for him."

"What for?"

"I've been hearing rumors it was *Tech* who
jumped the abyss, and was responsible for the
Netquake."

"What it if was?"

"Seeing is believing, Marz. Let's see him prove
it."

"Jump it yourself!"

Bios7 snorted. "You can seriously look me in
the craft and say that? You've got nerve, just
like your pilot bud. But you can tell Tech for me
that the next time I see him, I'm going to drag
his sorry butt over to the Escarpment and *make*
him jump—or should I say fall?"

"I'll be sure to tell him," Marz said.

"And here's something for *you* to think about:
You're not the only one who can design custom
craft. In fact, your days as top dog are over."

Marz worked his jaw. "We'll see what's what
the next time we meet."

He shut off the audio link and began downloading code signatures of the shapeshifter, determined to assimilate as much data as he could. It irked him that Bios7 had somehow gained access to software of an obviously whole new variety; and it irked him more that not one ship in the garage would stand a chance against Bios7's shapeshifter—even with Tech at the helm.

*I'm going to find out where you got the software to build that craft, Bios7,* Marz promised himself. *And I'm going to build Tech a better and faster one.*

## Chapter 5

WEB WARRIORS

"With CiscoSoft Entertainment's gratitude for preventing what could have been a promotional nightmare," Ralph Sweaps said as he handed a check across the desk to Felix.

"We aims to please!" Tech and Marz said, like a pair of jabbering blackbirds. They traded glances and smiled, yesterday's argument dissolving instantly. Tech gave Marz an affectionate tap on the upper arm.

Sweaps glanced at the boys and grinned, in no detectable way put off by their youth or irreverence. He was a lean, good-looking guy in his late thirties, wearing a $1,000 suit and a pair of $500 tassel-toed leather shoes. He was so unlike the dark-shaded, junk food–fed loonies who usually found their way to the Data Discoveries waiting room that Felix had initially feared that Sweaps had walked into the wrong office by mistake, or worse, that he was a NetSec agent.

His business card identified him as an executive producer—and lawyer. That Sweaps should condescend to pay Data Discoveries a personal visit instead of simply phoning suggested that CiscoSoft Entertainment was very pleased indeed to have Marty Morph back where he belonged.

Felix stared at the amount written on the check and whistled softly. "Extremely generous," he said. "It's going to look good for Data Discoveries to land a major client. NetTV'll be all over the story."

Sweaps tipped his head to one side in uncertainty.

"Maybe we should consider a photo op to show you presenting me with this check," Felix said, thinking out loud. "Or some CiscoSoft honcho thanking us for rescuing Marty Morph . . ."

Felix allowed his words to trail off when he saw the frown forming on Sweap's tanned face.

"Sorry, McTurk," he said, shaking his head, "but that's not possible."

Felix blinked in confusion. "But, but you said yourself that we saved CiscoSoft's—"

"And you did. But publicity's the last thing we want. Marty's in for rehab programming. He's had some problems in the past, and we can't have anyone looking into that. In fact, the sooner this little episode is put behind us, the better."

Felix traded stunned looks with Tech and Marz, then scratched his head. "How about an Internet story?"

Sweaps stared at him in disbelief. "For crying out loud, McTurk, we're not just talking about any toon. We're talking about Marty Morph. We're talking about a franchise worth over a billion dollars in licensing and endorsements alone. Do you have any idea what could become of that if Marty's millions of fans realized that their star had been responsible for knocking thousands of fliers off-Network and single-handedly crashing more than twenty Net sites?"

"You want this swept under the carpet," Felix said, stone-faced.

"Under the carpet, then you drop a building on it, then you bury everything under however much concrete it takes. Am I making myself clear?"

Felix flicked the check with the back of his fingertips. "Crystal."

Sweaps spread his manicured hands. "Listen, McTurk. I'm a reasonable guy. I think I know a way we can make each other happy."

"This better be good," Marz muttered.

Sweaps threw him a grin, then crossed his legs and looked at Felix. "You've heard about *Cyberchallenge*?"

Felix shook his head.

"The unreality show," Tech said. "Everyone's heard of it. Make it through some hostile cyberscapes, then team up to build the ultimate racing craft."

Marz leaned forward with interest, but didn't say anything about his friend Ramlock being a contestant.

"CiscoSoft Entertainment has a lot riding on the show," Sweaps continued. "We don't want to see the same thing happen to *Cyberchallenge* that happened to Marty Morph."

"I get it," Felix said. "But you still haven't told us what caused Marty to embark on his little Net binge."

Sweaps nodded. "I'm no technopath, McTurk, so I can't give you the zeros and ones on this. But our cyberspecialists think that Marty's escape had something to do with the creative neural net computer we recently installed to write Marty's scripts and oversee our NetTV programming."

"You think your neural net's glitched?" McTurk asked.

Sweaps nodded his head from side to side. "It's possible that it wrote Marty a script that took him into the Network. But there's a second, and more troubling possibility."

"Cyber-sabotage," Felix said. "Carried out by CiscoSoft's competition in the entertainment industry."

Sweaps was impressed. "First they try to embarrass us by infecting Marty Morph. Now we're worried they'll attempt to ruin the debut of *Cyberchallenge* by getting to the neural net a second time."

"You want us to check out the neural net?" Marz asked.

Sweaps shook his head. "I'd like you to attend the *Cyberchallenge* launch party undercover, and make certain that no one is messing with the neural net, either remotely or by any other method."

"Security?" Marz said in agitated disappointment. "You want us to run cyber-security?"

"Welcome to the bottom of the cyber-barrel," Tech muttered.

Sweaps shrugged. "You'll be on hand for a great party at Lot 49. Tons of Net stars."

"Virt Pam?" Tech asked excitedly.

"I think Virt Pam could be there." Sweaps turned to Felix. "What do you say, McTurk? Do we have a deal?"

"Take it, Felix," Tech urged. "We'll do the undercover work."

Felix raised a finger in warning. "No Virt Pam, is that understood?"

Tech frowned. "I guess."

Felix looked at Sweaps. "We'd need to know a lot more about the neural net that's running the show. You said it was a recent installation. Who's the maker?"

"A company called Mach Two."

Felix, Tech, and Marz exchanged covert glances of sudden surprise.

An open secret to those in the know, Mach Two was a front company for Peerless Engineering.

Darkness was gathering over the Colorado Rockies when Skander Bulkroad met with the twelve members of his board of directors. This was not the governing body of Bulkroad's multinational corporation, Peerless Engineering, but his cabal of silent partners in the secret business of reshaping the real and virtual worlds.

Their place of conclave was Bulkroad's mountain retreat, a sprawling medieval fortress that had been the inspiration for the castle that dominated the Network. Disassembled in its native France and transported in pieces to a huge tract of land southwest of Loveland, the castle had expanded over the years, in keeping with the success and expansion of Peerless Engineering itself. As it had grown, so too had its Network analog, until—except for their settings—there was almost no telling them apart.

The board room was three stories high and a hundred feet long. Medieval tapestries fell from the exposed beam ceiling, adding more warmth to the room's cut-stone chill than did the fireplace, which was spacious enough to accommodate a pair of midsize sedans. A pyramidal arrangement of enormous flatscreen monitors displayed images transmitted from remote areas of the castle where the workers toiled, stationed at their keyboards and cyberdecks, enslaved to code, sustaining and policing the nether-realm Peerless had brought into being—the unreal estate of the Virtual Network.

In the fervid glow of torchlight, attendants sworn to silence served food and drinks to the conspirators, who sat at a round wooden table believed to be an exact duplicate of King Arthur's, and carved from the world's last old-growth mahogany tree. Bulkroad—a rotund man with blunt features and a shiny dome of a head—sat in his customary armchair, with all eyes trained on him. Even ten years later, he was still getting used to the unwavering allegiance of his gang of twelve. Who knew what Peerless might have been able to accomplish had he known such loyalty when the company was just another startup, a tiny blip on the stock market? But what amazed him was that the best was yet to come—for Skander Bulkroad, and for Peerless.

"The damage sustained by the Peerless Castle during the Netquake and aftershocks has been repaired," one of the twelve was saying—a tall and gaunt man who spoke with a trace of Eastern European accent. "But it is important to keep in mind that a quake of equal or greater magnitude could result in irreparable damage, not only to the castle, but also to the Project. Therefore, I urge that we complete the proposed expansion into the Wilds as quickly as possible, and relocate the domain permanently."

The woman seated to the man's left took over. As close to faultless as the man was flawed, she had radiant blond hair and eyes that shone like emeralds. Her name was Eva.

"The domain's current permeability leaves it vulnerable to attack, much more so than when its only entry point was concealed inside the castle, and under our supervision and control."

"And yet, even then the domain was penetrated," the youngest of the twelve said. In sharp contrast to Eva, she had a sunken face and a mane of lackluster brown hair. Like others seated at the table, she was thin to the point of raw-boned, and almost too ghastly to look at.

"What took place two weeks ago was not unanticipated," the first man argued, "and should not reflect adversely on those responsible for maintaining security."

Eva looked hard at Bulkroad. "We must act now to seize the code sequence that enabled the boy to execute his jump from the Escarpment. Once we have that sequence, our expansion into the Wilds will be an accomplished fact, and the sleepers can be permanently relocated, without further security concerns."

"How do you envision this expansion being achieved?" Bulkroad asked the slender · man seated at his right, a technopath named Yob.

"A suspension bridge can be constructed along the code course of the flight plan," Yob said in a sniffling voice. "A bridge will have the added benefit of completing the design of the Network itself, making it possible for the in-migration of tens of thousands of new arrivals."

"We're fortunate that the cybernaut who made the jump has not repeated his act and initiated a second Netquake," an aged man at the far end of the table said. "I agree with Welkin, that another rend in the carefully maintained unreality of the Network could be catastrophic."

"All credit to the warning we issued the boy," Welkin said, in thick accent.

"I'm not convinced that that warning has anything to do with his not jumping," Yob said, between laborious breaths. "As recently as yesterday afternoon, he was observed at the Escarpment. He has attempted to cloak the signatures of his various craft, but we know who he is—both in cyberspace and in what passes here for 'real life.' "

"Jesse Vega," Welkin said. "Known in the Network as 'Tech.' I concur with Eva and Agrew that Tech must be apprehended, so that we may get on with the business of extracting the information he contains."

"He's just a boy," Bulkroad said. He leaned forward, resting his elbows on the table. "Frankly, I'm more interested in apprehending Cyrus than I am this Tech. Harwood Strange was certainly the person who provided Tech with the jump codes, but Cyrus is the real danger. He must be flushed from hiding and recaptured, before it's too late."

"The path to one is the path to the other," the long-haired Eva said carefully, "since it was Tech who was partially involved in Cyrus' resurrection, and Tech who, previous to jumping the abyss, twice penetrated the domain. Tech and Cyrus are operating out of the octagonal construct Cyrus originally constructed to harbor himself, and now functions as the Network office for the cyberdetective company known as Data Discoveries."

Bulkroad heard her out before replying. "If

Cyrus no longer resides in the octagon, what machines is he using to support his continued presence in the Network?"

Yob spoke to the question. "It is our assumption that those machines are housed at Data Discoveries, in Manhattan. They are obviously not stand-alone machines, or resurrected Cyrus would not have Network access. As a cyberentity, he comports himself as a program gremlin, but I am certain that he would prove to be a much more elusive target than Tech."

"We would do better to sabotage Cyrus' machines," Welkin said. "We simply need a way into the machines—by modem, or through the Network."

"Too risky," Eva countered. "We must somehow lure Cyrus back into his octagon in the Wilds, where he can be attacked by more conventional means."

"Are we so certain that Cyrus is a danger to us?" Agrew asked from the far end of the table. "Cyrus was successful in retrieving the parts of himself he copied and uploaded into the EPA, Worldwide Cellular, and other Network sites. But we know for a fact that he was only partially successful in retrieving the memories he concealed in the Peerless library databanks. And those memories are crucial to his understanding of the Project, and the reason for his termination."

"I know him like a father knows a son," Bulkroad said bluntly, "and I can assure you that even without those memories Cyrus is a danger to all of us. He must be silenced."

A foreboding voice interrupted from the velvet shadows at the rear of the board room. "It was my duty to watch for and prevent Cyrus' resurrection. I failed you."

With wet sucking breaths, a brittle articulation of decaying joints, a click-clack sound—like talons striking stone—the owner of the voice advanced into less dense shadow. There, the flickering torchlight revealed a hawkish profile, parched skin drawn tight across angular bones, an ugly decurved slash of mouth.

"Good to have you back, Scaum," Bulkroad said, with a touch of displeasure. "It appears that your reassembly was . . . successful."

"Don't be fooled by appearances," Scaum rasped. "A vessel may appear undamaged, and yet its contents may be spoiled."

Bulkroad gestured broadly. "Several of your comrades have been employing loaner vessels to good effect. You might consider doing the same."

Scaum ignored the advice. "The Project," he said.

"Your brief absence was a temporary setback. At great expense—and at the risk of touching off a second Netquake—we were forced to rewrite and relocate the domain. But we're back on track now."

"And my comrades in the Network?"

"Flourishing. Although I expect you to persuade them to exercise greater self-control. I can understand their eagerness to be themselves again, after so long a confinement. But their reckless actions jeopardize the Project."

Scaum snarled. "You must provide us with the room to expand. That was our arrangement, was it not?"

Bulkroad's eyes flashed in anger. "Peerless is working on its end of the deal. But we mustn't work at cross purposes, Scaum. Recently one of your comrades took it upon himself to seize hold of an entertainment program and throw the Network into chaos, rather than to remain lodged where he was to serve our mutual goals. Not realizing who he was, Peerless Castle security nearly disabled him. In the end it didn't matter, since he was forced to jettison at the last moment, or risk being snared by a group of pursuers."

"What pursuers?"

"The team at Data Discoveries," Bulkroad said, his anger undiminished, "which now includes resurrected Cyrus."

Scaum advanced further into the light, startling everyone but Bulkroad to rigidity.

"You leave Cyrus to me."

## Chapter 6

WEB WARRIORS

"Bios7 is online," Cyrus said to Tech, Marz, and Isis.

The three of them had just begun to strategize on how best to run cyber-security for CiscoSoft Entertainment. Isis had perked up at mention of the fact that the *Cyberchallenge* launch party was to be held at Lot 49, the hippest of Manhattan's newest clubs.

"You sure it's Bios7?" Marz asked Cyrus from his seat at the cyberdeck console.

"The signature I'm monitoring matches the one you provided me for Bios7 shapeshifter craft."

Tech was already settling into the dentist's chair when Isis said, "Hold on a minute. We're supposed to be working. And the job has nothing to do with trailing Tech's competition for 'Fastest Nerd on the Net.'"

"Ha, ha," Tech said. He tossed Isis a headset. "Consider this practice for keeping tabs on CiscoSoft's neural net. Besides, there's new soft to test out."

"Chameleon soft," Marz said. "Totally boot."

Isis scowled at the brothers. "Do you ever run anything that's legally published?"

"Not if we can help it," Tech said.

Tech and Isis went in undercover, running silent in low-profile black lozenges, called Cloaks. The Chameleon soft allowed the Cloaks to blend mimetically with their surroundings, and to emit only the faintest of signatures.

Every so often the multinational corporations that administered and financed the Network— companies like Peerless Engineering, Mitsuni, and Einstaad-Cordova—sponsored what had come to be called "Event Days." You might log on to find the Ribbon bedecked with holiday lights, or the virtual sky orange rather than blue, or CyberSquare transformed into an arts and craft fair. Today, though, the Net bigwigs, the "chefs of code," had eclipsed the sun, filled the virtual air with drizzle, and slicked the grid's highways and cross-streets with pools of dark water. So as it happened, Marz's Cloaks were the perfect craft for following Bios7 through a darkened cyberspace.

"Remember to give him plenty of lead, and to keep your headlamps damped down," Marz said, after Cyrus had suggested a good place for picking up Bios7's trail.

Tech, Isis, and the AI were concealed in a deeply shadowed alleyway that meandered through Sublevel Three's cyberdocks and warehouses. Less than a minute passed before Marz sent them an alert, and Bios7's shapeshifter drifted past their hiding place.

"That's totally whacked!" Tech gasped when he got a look at the craft.

"Have you ever seen anything like that before?" Marz asked.

"Never."

"Not even on my uncle's screens," Isis added, equally stunned.

"Cyrus?" Marz said.

The AI took a moment to reply. "I seem to recall something . . ."

The trio nosed their Cloaks out of the alleyway and accelerated, even while taking care to afford Bios7 as much maneuvering room as he needed.

The renowned racer led them up through Sublevels Two and One—the shapeshifter's pulsating running lights saturating the shallow rain puddles with reflected color—and finally onto the principal horizontal axis of the grid, some forty blocks cyber-west of the Ribbon, itself a river of streaming lights. In patches of low-lying fog, the shapeshifter was a muted gem, backlighting the mist with kaleidoscopic displays of color.

Still, Bios7 flew conservatively, refraining from putting his craft through any of the contour changes he had taken it through to impress the fliers at Ziggy's.

"He's heading south toward the Escarpment," Marz updated.

"And picking up speed," Isis said.

"Warp Seven—engage!" Tech said.

They accelerated to tighten the gap. Then, all at once the shapeshifter shot far into the lead, raising turbulent wakes in the puddles and executing whiplash turns that would have sent ordinary craft sliding out of control.

"He's going evasive on us," Isis said.

Tech snorted. "You keeping him in your sights, Cyrus?"

"Yes. His maneuvers are well within my capacity to process."

"That's encouraging," Marz said, " 'cause I'm having trouble keeping track of him. Ripper is loading in case you need a velocity boost."

"Isis?" Tech asked.

"Do it!"

Propelled by a sudden surge of power, he and Isis raced under a series of low overpasses and through a darkened intersection. Sluing through a tight turn, they caught sight of the shapeshifter's running lights retreating at incalculable speed.

A laugh of ridicule cut through the thick silence of their audio link. Then Bios7's voice filled their headphones.

"What a bunch of washouts! Did you really think you could stalk me without my knowing? Cloaks are so last decade. And I see you've brought reinforcements, Marz. That's gotta be Tech in one of the other Cloaks. Who's the gonad helming the program gremlin?"

"Gonad?" Cyrus said, mostly to himself.

"Hey, Tech," Bios7 went on, "did Marz give you my message?"

"Yeah, I got it."

"Too bad there isn't time to haul you over to the abyss, but I've got pressing business with my new software suppliers. I'm sure there'll be other opportunities."

"Tech looks forward to it, weenie," Isis said.

"A female," Bios7 said in surprise. "Congratulations on entering puberty, boys."

"We'll be sure to let you know how it is," Tech said. "Meanwhile, we'll just keep riding your tail."

"Suit yourselves."

Anticipating Bios7, Tech and Isis poured on speed, but the shapeshifter managed to maintain its lead. Even Cyrus was straining to keep up. Tech's nemesis led them on a merry chase over narrow bridges, through unlighted tunnels, and down one path in the wrong direction. Closing fast on the western terminus of the Escarpment, he teased and tweaked them, leading them through power climbs and spiraling descents.

"Power drain," Isis asked breathlessly. "Shields buckling. I don't know how much more of this we can take!"

"Marz, you gotta give us more speed!" Tech said.

"Turbo is booting up on the auxiliary deck," Marz replied. "It might not be compatible with Ripper."

"We'll take the chance."

*"Whooaa!"* Isis said as Turbo fired up. "Marz, dial down my capture vest! I'm dropping out!"

"I got you, Isis. Slow down, Tech!"

"No way!"

The pulsing shapeshifter was suddenly back in sight, with Tech's Cloak rapidly closing Bios7's lead. Ahead of them lay the shallow end of the Escarpment, and the Wilds beyond.

"We got him now," Tech said. "He's trapped."

"Isis, you okay?" Marz asked.

"Isis who?" she started to say, when Tech broke in.

"He's changing vectors again!"

Before the words had left his mouth, the shapeshifter powered through an unexpected turn. But by the time Tech and Cyrus, and, finally, Isis rounded the same corner, Bios7 had disappeared.

Tech took his Cloak through a series of confused circles. "Where'd he go, Cyrus?"

"I'm not sure, Tech. Perhaps he went into the Wilds."

"But he turned away from the Escarpment," Isis pointed out.

"I don't get this," Tech said. "What'd he do, make the jump to lightspeed or something?"

"Maybe he went off-line," Isis suggested.

"No," Marz said, "he's still logged on."

"Then why can't we see him, bro?" Tech brought his Cloak to a halt. "There must be some kind of entry or exit portal around here. Spread out and search every nook and cranny of this place."

They were on the verge of doing just that when the audio link came alive once more, and Felix's voice boomed in everyone's ears.

"Guys, Cyrus," Felix said. "Ease up on the CiscoSoft security prep for a while."

"Oh, yeah, CiscoSoft," Marz said. "We were, uh, about to take a break anyway."

"I'm in Harwood's room at the hospital."

"Oh, no," Isis said. "Bad news?"

"Just the opposite. Get over here right now."

One of the shabbiest medical facilities in Manhattan, Shady Grove was deep in the Bronx, a long subway ride from both Data Discoveries and the Safehaven Group Home.

When it had become clear to everyone that Harwood's comatose condition could persist for months, or even years, Felix had arranged to have Harwood Strange moved there from the uptown hospital to which he had been admitted originally. Since residing in the medcenter, Harwood had shown no improvement. He remained as unresponsive as he had been after losing to Scaum, in the heart of the Peerless Castle.

Once known to millions of interactive-music fans as "Mystery Notes," the former composer and outlaw hacker who had helped the Vega brothers unravel the mystery of Cyrus lay on his back in the oversize bed the medcenter had provided, a white sheet pulled up to his chin, with his beard resting outside it like a glacier moving down from the craggy face above.

Getting a gander at that neatly shaped but

ever lengthening beard as he entered Harwood's room, Marz muttered to Tech, "Rip Van Winkwood."

A bank of machines beeped and chirped in the background, and at the foot of the bed stood Felix and an exceedingly tall and pasty-faced man, sporting a white lab coat that dropped nearly to his ankles and a pair of enormous, and highly incongruous, black-framed sunglasses. On his sunken right cheek was a blue spot that might have been a birthmark.

Felix caught sight of the three teens, and swung to them, at the same time motioning to the pale beanpole beside him. "This is Dr. Matterling, from the Ravenston Clinic in . . ."

"Baltimore."

"Baltimore," Felix repeated. "Dr. Matterling, meet Isis, Tech, and his brother Marz—"

"You two are brothers?" Matterling broke in, peering at them over the tops of the shades.

Tech waved a courtly gesture to Marz—their signal that it was his turn to provide the usual rejoinder.

"We were designed to be different."

"Evidently."

"Dr. Matterling has taken an interest in Harwood," Felix continued, "and I wanted you to hear what he has to say."

Marz and Isis plopped themselves down on the foot of the bed. Tech remained standing.

Wearing a long, metallic-fabric coat, amber-tinted goggles with attached earphones, and a sensor-studded data glove on his right hand,

Tech figured he must have looked as peculiar to Matterling as Matterling looked to him. The various items were all part of a wireless-interface cyborg suit, which allowed him to inhabit the real world and the Network simultaneously.

Parts of the rig were prototypes Isis had liberated from her uncle's cyber-research lab; other parts were prizes Tech and Marz had won in Network contests, for extreme sports racing and craft-design respectively. Tech didn't wear the rig often, and it might have been easier to have carted along a portable videophone, but the suit was the surest way of permitting Cyrus to eavesdrop on whatever was about to go down.

"The reason I've taken a keen interest in your friend's dilemma," Matterling said with a thick European accent, "is because I've had success in the past with scores of similar cases."

"You mean you can wake Harwood up?" Marz said.

"I believe so."

"How do you do it?" Isis asked.

"By taking my patients back into the Network."

Felix and the three teens traded uneasy looks. Tech was first with the question all of them were pondering.

"How can you take a comatose person into the Network?"

Matterling regarded Tech for a long moment before responding. "Strictly speaking, Mr. Strange is not in a coma. His condition is closer to that of a fugue state, where trauma has resulted in his consciousness being trapped in a loop. Think of it as a dream from which you can't awaken. Research suggests that cyberflying relies heavily on the older, reptilian functions of our brains, as opposed to the higher centers of awareness. Because of this, lost cyberfliers like Mr. Strange can often be brought out of their fugue states, their dream states, by just the sort of optic nerve stimulation afforded by the Virtual Network."

Felix firmed his lips and shook his head. "Sure, you can put a headset and a motion-capture vest on Harwood. But I don't see how you're going to get him to operate a joystick and navigate the Network when he can't even blink his eyes."

"Unnecessary," Matterling said, "since I will serve as his navigator." Taking a remote control from the deep pocket of his lab coat, he turned and called to his side a wheeled table, atop of which sat a large, helmetlike device. "The immersion globe—my own invention—is equipped with the equivalent of a data-display visor. Once it is fitted over Mr. Strange's head, appliances inside will pry and keep open his eyelids."

"In there?" Marz said, gulping as he pointed to the sinister-looking globe. "Harwood's head goes in *there*?"

Matterling regarded him flatly. "It's painless, I assure you. Ideally, I would like to return him to the Network site where he suffered the original trauma. Perhaps you could furnish me with the

Network Positioning coordinates where the tragic event occurred."

Tech cringed. They couldn't very well confess that Harwood had lost his mind inside the Peerless Castle—not without explaining about the hidden domain he and Tech had discovered, and about Scaum.

"Uh, I don't think that's going to be possible," Tech said when no one else spoke. "See, we're not really sure where it happened . . ."

"Not a problem," Matterling said, waving his thin-fingered hand. "The Network is rich in stimulating places. I'm certain I can find one that will suffice to awaken Mr. Strange." He paused briefly. "Under normal circumstances, Mr. Strange's family members would have to give their permission for such a procedure to be performed. But since you are the people responsible for his treatment, the decision rests with you."

"There's really a chance?" Felix asked.

Matterling nodded. "I would be glad to provide you with the names of several patients who have been awakened, and gone on to lead normal lives."

The room fell silent, save for the monitoring machines.

Tech was gazing at Harwood when Cyrus—as gremlin—suddenly appeared in the right lens of his tinted goggles.

"Tech, I've corroborated Dr. Matterling's credentials," Cyrus said into Tech's headset earphones. "Give him whatever permission he needs.

Besides, Shady Grove is accessible by way of the Network, so I can easily infiltrate the medcenter's monitoring machines—perhaps even the navigation helmet Matterling proposes to use—and make certain that Mystery Notes isn't placed in further jeopardy."

Tech reached surreptitiously into his antennae-impregnated jacket and typed a response into the chording keyboard strapped around his waist.

*What about the security detail for* Cyberchallenge?

"I will provide Marz with everything he needs to monitor CiscoSoft's neural net for any signs of remote infiltration or sabotage," Cyrus said into Tech's right ear. "Trust me, Tech. It's more important that I watch over Mystery Notes for the time being."

Looking at Harwood with his left eye and Cyrus with his right, Tech nodded discreetly.

*You know what's best.*

## Chapter 7

WEB WARRIORS

Standing shoulder to shoulder with Isis, his head thrown back and his eyes trained upward, Tech figured that he could be looking at the night sky overhanging a desert, or somewhere on planet Earth where the air was clear. Slowly, though, the stars and planets, the spiral galaxies and golden comets began to disperse and rearrange themselves, until they had coalesced in dazzling holographic cursive to form the word: *Cyberchallenge*.

With that the hundreds of invited guests in the hemispherical main room of Lot 49 went crazy, cheering and applauding. Fiber-optic fireworks crazed the dome's false sky and the sweep of stars that had been the Milky Way began to shower down as colored-foil confetti. Strobe and spotlights played over the crowd, and bouquets of phosphorescent helium balloons rose toward the ceiling. Remote cameras sent close headshots to the club's fifty huge and seemingly free-floating display screens. The voice of a velvet-throated DJ stretched the show's title to twice its syllabic length, and dance mix boomed from banks of overhead and floor-level speakers.

"How cool is this?" Isis said, yelling to be heard, even though her lips were only inches from Tech's left ear.

"Bah," he yelled back. "The music sucks and I *hate* crowds."

"Come on, let's get closer to the stage," Isis said, already pulling him along, and this time relying on her tiny, stalked microphone to convey the words directly to Tech's earphones.

Both of them were wearing minimal wireless-interface suits. But what with all the dance freaks, the fashion models, and the handheld-camera and Network lens operators, they were just two more oddballs in the crowd.

As they wormed their way toward the circular platform in the center of the club, Tech watched her move to the music, gracefully and sensually. He was still staring at her when Isis reached for his hand, and he recoiled, as if stung.

"Are you okay?" she asked.

"Why wouldn't I be?" Tech said without looking at her.

"I don't know. You've been kinda jumpy lately. Are you worried about Harwood?"

" 'Course I am."

"Cyrus is looking after Harwood. Everything'll

be fine." She studied him for a moment. "How'd you get that black-'n'-blue on your cheek?"

Tech frowned. "Minor dustup at Safehaven."

"With who? Don't tell me Fidelia knocked you one!"

Tech smiled. "Just some dork."

Isis shook her head. "Can't you and Marz leave that place? I mean, why doesn't Felix just adopt you or something?"

"Yeah, maybe."

"You guys practically live at Data Discoveries already."

Tech cracked a smile. "At least with Felix I'll only be losing my privileges every *other* weekend."

"You might even be able to get out and catch a movie—like a regular person."

"In the real world?" Tech asked in dramatic distress. "I'd need to give that some thought."

They had managed to advance a good thirty feet when *Cyberchallenge*'s host of ceremonies came onstage, to deafening applause. Telegenically handsome, he had succeeded in cultivating a manner that was at once agreeable and sociopathically cruel. He spent a long moment basking in the attention of the crowd before introducing the show's contestants—by their Network user names—and bringing them onstage. Some bowed, others acted completely unfazed, and a few clasped their hands over their heads in victory displays.

The contestants, too, seemed to have come

straight from reality-show central casting, and were therefore in no way representative of the cybercommunity to which the show was attempting to appeal, wherein anonymity and deception were prized. Instead, *Cyberchallenge*'s forty exemplified a multiethnic TV/Netcast contestant cross-section, with plenty of fit and bright-smiled twentysomethings, several middle-aged moms and dads, and a few out of shape or ill-tempered old dudes.

Their fans, however, displayed the kind of fervent following Tech associated with professional wrestling. Almost everyone in the crowd was dressed in or flying the colors of their chosen champions, and rhythmically hooting or raising fists into the air as they were introduced.

"Next, from Manhattan, New York," the emcee was saying, "a cyberdesigner and former all-state quarterback, who's just waiting for Hollywood to knock on his door . . . Ladies and gentlemen, meet Ramlock!"

"Whoo hoo, Ramlock!" Isis cheered.

Tech snorted a laugh as Ramlock stepped from the wings, dressed in bicycle tights and a Spandex top plastered with the logos of his corporate sponsors. "Looks like a fashion runway reject," he sent to Isis.

"Not!" she said, without taking her eyes from the stage. "He's cute!"

"Insert tongue back in mouth."

Isis turned, grinned, and smacked him in the upper arm. "Like you didn't drool over Virt Pam."

Tech rubbed his biceps. "Virt Pam is a goddess.

Besides, at least I do most of my panting in private."

"And now to introduce the real star of the show," the emcee went on when the crowd had quieted somewhat. "He helped to create the show, select the contestants, and plan the cyber-challenges—Obstacle Course, House of Horrors, Alien Encounter, and the rest. He's the gamemaster of guile, the ringmaster of risk, the arbiter of audacious action, from whom you'll be hearing a lot more as the show progresses, and whose decision will be final in all cases. Mee-eee-eet *Just-ice*!"

Gesturing broadly, the emcee pivoted 180 degrees, and there, released from whatever holo-magic had kept it concealed, stood a gargantuan, bipedal robot, whose strobing red eyes, though obviously meant to be menacing, came across like out-of-synch traffic signals.

Isis aimed her code scanners at the towering, two-legged machine and spent a moment studying the results.

Tech was shaking his head in amusement. "I can't believe Cisco would resort to a robot."

"That's CiscoSoft's neural net."

"Huh?"

"Inside the 'bot is the neural net we're supposed to be watching."

Tech stared openmouthed at the machine. "Yeah, I knew that." He paused, then laughed. "Now if they could just get the thing to touch its nose and rub its belly at the same time they'd really have something."

Isis continued to dance in place. "What do we do now?"

"Our job. We keep our electronic eyes and ears open. It's possible that hackers have been tampering with the neural net by remote. Felix thinks they might have been hired by a rival entertainment company, and that they could be inside the club." Tech glanced at her. "Set your rig to active mode."

Isis maneuvered the fingers of her sequined data glove. "I'm good to go."

Tech moved his microphone closer to his mouth. "Marz, are you there?"

A sleek, cylindrical craft—Terminator— resolved in the right lens of Tech's interface goggles. "Perimeter secure," Marz answered from cyberspace.

"How're you reading us?" Tech asked.

"Your signal's weak," Marz said. "Set your rig to send what you say as text, so we can save bytes."

"Did you get that?" Tech asked Isis.

"Text translator enabled, Marz."

"It's working," Marz said. "I heard you, and I'm reading what you say on my display screen. Are you picking up any remote interference in the club? Any signals aimed at the neural net?"

"The neural net is named Justice," Isis said.

"Negative for signal interference," Tech said. "All quiet."

"Suppose we do pick up something?" Isis asked. "What then?"

"We're only supposed to locate the source of

the signals," Marz said. "Felix doesn't want us to attempt any countermeasures."

"Marz, I'm picking up a data spike!" Tech said.

"Something weird's going on," Marz said. "A huge cybercraft just exited CiscoSoft's Network site. It's a program—launched by Justice!"

Tech glanced at the giant robot that housed the powerful quantum computer. "Launched deliberately or escaped?"

"I'm not sure," Marz said. "But the program just roared right past me. It's dressed in space shuttle software. Should I follow it?"

"Heck, yes, you should follow it," Tech started to say, when Cyrus suddenly replaced Marz's Terminator in Tech's Network-active display window.

"Tech!" the program gremlin said in a rush.

"What? I'm kinda busy—"

"It would be best if you could come to Shady Grove immediately!"

Tech showed Isis a wide-eyed look of uncertainty. "What should I do?"

"Go," she said. "I'll continue sweeping for any unusual signals here, and keep the link open to Marz in the Network."

Tech nodded and pulled off his headset. "I'll call you from the medcenter as soon as I know anything."

For a vintage ship, the space shuttle could really *move*.

Lifting off from CiscoSoft's Network complex,

a couple of blocks north of CyberSquare, it climbed rapidly above the Ribbon, continuing to gain altitude until it was five levels above the commercial district, where it leveled off and headed to a south-southwesterly course, toward the Escarpment. Marz could keep up with the ship, but only because the Terminator was running a Ziggy's-special version of Turbo.

Why CiscoSoft's neural net would be launching a program of such size and speed was anyone's guess; unless, of course, the neural net was glitched, as Felix suspected, or the unexpected takeoff was the work of cyber-operatives hoping to sabotage the debut of *Cyberchallenge*. Still, how had they managed to infiltrate the neural net, and what was the destination of the space shuttle?

Still high over the Ribbon, it was moving at remarkable speed compared to the traffic, which was mostly made up of government-issue podcraft heading to and from Level Five's heavily patrolled administrative and municipal districts. Marz was worried that Network Security would appear at any moment and put a premature end to the chase—and the mystery—either by trying to intercept the space shuttle, or by whacking Marz's Terminator with a dose of arresting code for exceeding the posted speed limits.

Gradually, though, the surreptitious program began to descend back toward the Ribbon, shedding enough velocity as it fell to keep it safe from NetSec radar, as well as allow Marz not only to catch up, but also to enable Grappler, and *attach* the Terminator to the shuttle's dark underbelly.

In the Data Discoveries flight room, he lifted his feet from the dentist's chair's control pedals and let the joystick center itself in neutral. He was so accustomed to navigating for Tech and Isis—when she would let him, at any rate—that it bothered him to be leaving the flying to some-one else, particularly a possibly seriously glitched Mach Two neural net named Justice, of all things. But one thing was made abundantly clear: the program wasn't simply capering about, as, say, Marty Morph had done. In fact, the space shuttle seemed to know precisely where it was going. But it was only after it had crossed three-quarters of the grid, and the west-ern terminus of the Escarpment came into view, that Marz, too, had a uneasy feeling about its destination.

"Tech, Isis, where are you guys?" he asked over their dedicated audio link. "Are you in the Network or not?" When neither of them re-sponded, he hailed Cyrus, but to no avail.

Marz assumed that the AI was still monitoring Harwood at Shady Grove, but, for the life of him, he couldn't figure out why Tech and Isis weren't answering him. Something had to have come up in Lot 49 that prevented them from ac-cessing the Network. One possible cause would be signal interference or jamming by news or-ganizations that were covering the event live for various Network and TV shows. Even if Tech and Isis were online by now, it would be too late for them to catch up. But Marz would know exactly where to tell them to go as soon as they established contact, for the space shuttle was closing on the same area where Bios7 had disappeared the previous day!

From his perch beneath the prop plane, Marz scanned the surroundings. This far from the Ribbon, the sites were either private havens or quadrangular storage dumps, leased or owned by multinational corporations. Floating above one such dump, and unusual to encounter in such a bleak environment, was an advertising icon—a kind of billboard analog—that read: *"Live the future. Build your own condo in the Wilds."* What's more, the space shuttle was making no attempt to steer a course around the billboard. Instead, it had aligned itself with the second *o* in condo, and, seconds later, was flying straight through it, taking the attached Terminator along for the ride.

Marz's jaw fell open in astonishment.

Tech had been right.

The area in which Bios7's shapeshifter had disappeared housed a hidden gate—a *portal*!

Marz peered into gray fog that extended to all sides of him. The space shuttle had obviously entered some sort of transitional area, a cyber-limbo. But the shuttle hadn't traveled far when it came to a sudden halt, and a text message began to scroll across a display window in

Marz's visor—a message being transmitted to the space shuttle.

*An unregistered attachment has been detected. Please dump or delete attachment before proceeding.*

Marz muttered a curse of disappointment as the space shuttle jettisoned the Terminator, and he felt himself drift away. The space shuttle then advanced into the mist and vanished from sight. But things could have gone worse. At least the neural net program hadn't tried to delete him. Held immobile, he was trying to figure out what to do next when additional text appeared in the display window.

*You must register and upgrade your craft before being allowed to enter this domain. Do you wish to register and upgrade now?*

Caught in a quandary, Marz cursed again. If he waited for Tech and Isis to arrive, he could end up losing track of the space shuttle. But if he proceeded into the domain without them, it was unlikely that they would be able to contact him.

*Yes*, he typed at last. Then, when prompted to, he provided an identity and a Network address from a grab bag of counterfeits he and Tech made frequent use of.

*Registration complete. Stand by to receive upgrade options.*

Momentary flashes of intense light speared Marz's eyes, causing an uncomfortable tingling sensation at the back of his head. Then a series of incredible vessels began to resolve in midair in front of him: shapeshifters, like Bios7's, but also craft that resembled medieval weapons, architectural gargoyles, and other mythical beasts, modified to resemble cybercraft.

Marz thought for a long moment, then indicated a craft that resembled a spiked sphere. The code that held the craft together was complicated beyond his abilities to decipher.

*You have chosen Mace. Return in this craft as often as you wish, and be sure to check for further upgrades.*

Marz was astounded to see the Terminator morph and sprout clusters of short spikes.

Cautiously, he moved forward.

The gray fog began to grow patchy, then cleared completely, revealing a vast cityscape of towers and citadels, standing at odd angles to each other or pressed together like the peaks of a young mountain range. Many of them were encased in construction scaffolds, which gave them the look of medieval fortresses, piled high with parapets, bastions, and merlons. What constituted the sky was a swirl of murky colors, fractured by faraway strokes of lightning. A persistent sound like wind filled the headphones. Pointing and clicking on the scaffolded towers and other constructs yielded nothing more than a gibberish of letters—perhaps the impossible-to-pronounce names of foreign companies.

Marz recalled Tech's description of the domain he and Harwood Strange had discovered inside the Peerless Castle. Tech claimed to have seen jagged peaks rising from a whirlpooling carpet of electronic mist, and oily black presences that flowed and coiled like ink spilled into water. But there was none of that here.

He began to explore, pointing and clicking at random, and marveling at the new-generation craft that lazed or shot past him. Finally, he spied the space shuttle, linked to the tapered summit of a heavily-scaffolded construct, as if refueling through an extensible tether. Climbing that tether and disappearing into the fuselage of the plane were what looked like individual packets of black syrup.

Marz opened a link to Data Discoveries and tasked the office cybersystem to crosscheck the codes of the uploading packets. The system immediately informed him that the signatures of the packets were similar to that of the dark presence that had fled Marty Morph, on his being outsmarted in the Wilds.

So similar as to be nearly identical.

Marz reoriented his craft to face the citadel below. Pointing and clicking, he summoned data on the construct.

It had been built by Mach Two.

Working quickly, Marz launched and deployed Gobbler—a Pac-man-looking piece of software he and Tech had purchased at The Hackers Outlet. Tasking Gobbler to copy all novel code sequences, he began to upload as much information as he could carry. Then, when the space shuttle had completed loading, Marz maneuvered the Mace to within striking distance of the craft and reattached.

Bloated with uploaded code of its own, the ship returned to the hidden portal, and emerged from the cybercondo billboard into the Network. Once there, it slowly worked its way back to the Ribbon, making brief stops to download data at one or another corporate site. Then it proceeded back to CiscoSoft Entertainment, on the north side of CyberSquare, where it dumped the remainder of its puzzling cargo into Justice.

## Chapter 8

**WEB WARRIORS**

Harwood Strange was sitting up in bed. The machines that had kept careful track of his physical and cerebral functions had been disconnected, except for a remote pulse and blood pressure monitor that sheathed the forefinger of his left hand. In his right hand he held a tall glass of thick grass-green liquid Tech assumed was some sort of medicine. To one side of the bed stood skeletally thin Dr. Matterling; to the other, a female nurse, as bleached-looking as Matterling.

Gaping at Harwood, Tech tried to swallow the lump that had formed in his throat. Harwood looked painfully thin and sallow, but he was sitting up unassisted. Tech's eyes brimmed with tears.

"Mystery Notes," he blurted, dropping his Network interface jacket onto a chair as he ran into the room.

Matterling and the nurse turned in surprise. Matterling looked unhappy.

"Who notified you that Mr. Strange was awake?" he asked, with his thick, unplaceable accent.

"I, I was just in the neighborhood." Tech glanced at Harwood, and saw that the old man was staring at him.

Harwood raised his yellow-nailed left hand and pointed. "You, you're . . ."

Tech waited breathlessly.

"Give him a moment," Matterling cautioned. "He has only been awake for a couple of hours."

"Jesse," Harwood said at last.

Tech exhaled in jubilant relief and hurried to Harwood's side.

"Mystery Notes . . . Harwood . . . I can't believe it. You're *back*."

Harwood squinted at him, trying to recall something, then said, "Tech!"

Tech heard the pulse monitor begin to chirp more rapidly. Matterling moved Tech aside and leaned over Strange, pressing a stethoscope to Strange's rib cage.

"He's alarmed about something," Matterling said. "You shouldn't have visited so soon."

Tech started to apologize, when Harwood spoke again.

"Your brother . . . Marz."

Tech beamed, wiping tears from his eyes. "That's right. We took care of the cats for you."

Harwood's gaze became unfocused. "Cats?"

"Your cats, yeah. We had to find temporary homes for them."

"Thank you," Harwood said. He paused, then asked, "When did you and I meet? I can't seem to recall . . ."

Tech glanced at Matterling in confusion.

"Mr. Strange's memory of the events that resulted in his hospitalization is limited. But this is not unusual in recently awakened patients."

"Will he get his memory back?" Tech asked.

"It's impossible to say."

Tech looked at Harwood again. "You don't remember anything?"

Harwood tugged at his beard in reflection. "Cyrus . . ." he said vacantly.

Harwood was staring expectantly at Tech. "Did you find him?"

Tech's eyes darted between Harwood and Matterling. He didn't want to reveal any more than he had to, but he could sense Harwood's inner turmoil, and knew that he had to say something.

"Cyrus is alive, Mystery Notes."

Again the pulse monitor went wild, and the old man's eyes widened. "After all these years, Cyrus has resurfaced?"

Tech nodded. "But you might not recognize him as you, uh, remember him."

"Oh, I'm certain I'd recognize Cyrus anywhere. You must tell him that I'm eager to speak with him!"

Tech had his mouth open to respond, when Matterling put his bony hand on Tech's shoulder. "That's enough for now. You must give Mr. Strange sufficient time to adjust."

Tech stood up, nodding. "I'll see you soon, Mystery Notes."

"I look forward to hearing everything—Tech."

Tech scooped up his interface jacket and headset, slipping into the latter even as he was leaving the room. He was halfway down the mint-green corridor before he managed to contact Cyrus through the Network.

"Why did you take off your interface?" the AI asked in distress. "Why didn't you let me see and hear Mystery Notes for myself?"

"Harwood barely recognized me as it was. Imagine what he woulda thought if I'd been wearing the goggs and jacket."

"Does he remember what happened to him inside Peerless?" Cyrus went on. "Did he ask about me? Did you tell him that I want desperately to speak with him—"

"Whoa, hold your bytes, Cyrus! I told him about you—well, a little bit about you, anyway. He was definitely psyched to hear that you're all right—even though he doesn't realize you're not flesh and blood. He didn't remember anything about being inside Peerless, or going up against Scaum."

"That could complicate matters."

"He did remember Marz."

"Did he remember meeting Isis?"

"Isis!" Tech said. "I totally forget to call her! Cyrus, I'll get right back to you."

He enabled the wireless system's phone function and commanded it to speed dial Isis's cell phone number. She answered on the second ring.

"Data Discoveries. Isis here—*working*."

"I've just seen Harwood," Tech began. "His memory is shaky, but I think he's going to be all right."

"Great news! Where are you now?"

"Matterling didn't want me hanging around stressing Harwood out, so I split. Are you in touch with Marz?"

"I haven't been able to find him," Isis said in agitation. "I tried searching for him in the Net, but I couldn't pick up his course. Then I tried hailing him—and *you*—but neither of you answered. I don't know where Marz went, but I'm guessing he's still following the program that left the neural net, or he would have contacted me."

"Where are you now?" Tech said, jabbing at the elevator call button.

"Working security!" She exhaled in exasperation. "But the launch party's over. You missed everything!"

"Meet me back at HQ. Cyrus and I will try to locate Marz."

"Fine. But make sure to keep your cell phone on, in case I need to reach you."

Tech waited until the elevator had reached the medcenter's lobby before he lowered the goggles over his eyes and hailed Cyrus through the Network.

"Marz is missing," he began. "Isis figures he's in the Net, tailing a program that launched from CiscoSoft's neural net just before you called to tell us about Harwood. I'm gonna find a quiet corner and go active."

The medcenter lobby was empty, save for three workers in dark-blue utility coveralls, who were running polishing machines over the marble floor. Tech chose an out-of-the-way seat, close to the lobby's secondary entrance. The wireless rig's data goggles told him that he wasn't far from the medcenter's interface hub, which meant that he would be able to enter the Network via the nearby server rather than having to rely on tapping into Data Discoveries', across town.

Making himself comfortable in the faux-leather chair, Tech set the chording keyboard in his lap, selected a red Dino Ferrari from the portable deck's very restricted menu, and tasked both of the goggles' amber-tinted lenses to go Network-active. The Dino was a classic—with nowhere near the power of the 360 Spider—but it had sufficient tracking software for locating a missing or lost flier. With a lag Tech wasn't used to, the grid took shape below him, and, shortly, bright-blue Cyrus was alongside him.

"I've zeroed in on Marz's cybertrail," the AI said. "He headed toward the western terminus of the Escarpment, close to where we lost Bios7 yesterday."

"That's a long way for me to go in this rig," Tech said. "Can't do much speedboring on the medcenter's Network hub."

"I can assist."

"Do it."

Cyrus brought some of his crunching power to bear, molding a pair of tapered wings for the Dino and fueling it with high-octane booster code. Finally the gremlin and the modified Ferrari shot out over the Ribbon, angling for the express lanes. Well before the Peerless Castle, Tech and Cyrus veered southwest for the abyss, and the Wilds beyond.

When they had reached the western terminus of the digital divide, Tech took a long look around at the corporate storage dumps and private refuges. His eyes fell briefly on an advertisement for cybercondos in the Wilds.

"We're right back where we were yesterday," he said. "You sure you haven't confused Marz's course with Bios7's?"

"I'm certain."

"So where is he?"

"Give me a moment to calculate the possibilities."

"In other words, you're fresh out of ideas."

Tech deployed the Ferrari's software to home in on a craft matching the codes of Marz's Terminator. Flying in ever-expanding circles, he searched for additional signs of his brother's cyber-trail. He was close to the cybercondo advertisement when Cyrus hailed him.

"Tech, something's coming."

"What? Where?"

"Several unusual cybercraft are closing on us at rapid speed."

Tech scanned to the east. "The Ribbon off ramp is clear."

"Not from the Ribbon. Their launch point was in the Wilds."

"The Wilds?"

Tech swung the Dino about to face the Escarpment, and saw them leaping over the shallow terminus like a gang of Valkyries. Whoever the pilots were, they were flying a motley assortment of craft, with parts begged, borrowed, or stolen. In a glance, Tech spied grotesque fabrications of wheels and wings, bubble canopies and drive turrets, flags and banners, signs and sigils, radomes adorned with the toothy snarls of predators, or whiskered with weapons.

*Outlaws!*

Occupying the open cockpit of a chariot craft was a big, yapping dog, wearing flight goggles and a long black scarf.

"Cyrus, I don't have any weapons!"

"Then it's best to avoid them."

"Good idea."

Tech and Cyrus swerved northeast for the safety of the Ribbon, but the cyberoutlaws anticipated their course and intercepted them before they had gone a Network mile. Disabling code chased Tech's unresponsive craft, forcing it south, back toward the abyss, perhaps in the hope that he would ditch.

"The Dino's for show, not *go!*" Tech said,

wishing that Marz were navigating for him. Unless Tech could get clear, Data Discoveries' cybersystem was in jeopardy of being raided by the outlaws.

"Hold on, Tech."

Tech did what he could to avoid the salvos of disabling code, but the shaken Ferrari was already corrupted, and being reduced to a Volkswagen Beetle. He raced full out along the Escarpment's rim road, but there was no losing his assailants. They sent a chorus of frenzied hoots and yells into his headset earphones and began to form up on both sides of him. Then, firing flaming-arrow code that penetrated deeply into the thin skin of the show craft, the disparate craft circled him like Indian warriors surrounding a covered wagon.

"Cyrus!" Tech yelled, irked that he couldn't defend himself or escape.

He was bracing himself for a graceless exit when a giant blue dragon suddenly flew to his rescue, beating new-grown wings to disperse the circling warriors, and in the process absorbing megabytes of hostile code. Clutching what was now Tech's tricycle in a pair of family-size capture claws, the gremlin soared, leaving their unknown pursuers to rage and howl at their loss.

"Losing stability," Tech said hurriedly. "Code's almost played. Can you get me to an emergency exit?"

"There's one just ahead," Cyrus replied. "You'll have to perform an abbreviated exit. For your own sake, be as graceful as you can be."

Employing a technique known as "crisis decompression," Tech ran through a mental routine of calming exercises. When his eyepiece displays assured him that he had succeeded in returning his beta activity, blood pressure, and pulse rate to acceptable readings, he punched exit and logged out.

The lenses went to passive mode, and the medcenter lobby, amber-tinted by the goggles, spun round and round in front of his eyes. Sweating profusely under the interface jacket, Tech got shakily to his feet, and began to stagger for the nearest exit, his eyelids fluttering and his quivering hands stretched out in front of him.

Dizzy and nauseated, he was halfway to the revolving door when, out of the corner of his eye, he glimpsed two of the floor-polishers converging on him in a rush. For an instant, he thought they were coming to his aid.

Then he realized otherwise.

The last thing he saw were the glass panels of the door, spinning out of control.

Marz was seated at the Data Discoveries console when Isis exploded into the office.

"Where in the world have you been?" she said, glaring at him, red hair fanning around her face like flames.

"Off-world's more like it."

She threw her interface jacket and headset onto the couch. "Don't give me that, Marz. I'm in no mood."

He sent a scowl right back at her.

"I've been right here—well, in the Network, anyway. And where were you guys when I was tailing the neural net program? I waited for you as long as I could. Hey, why are you back here, anyway?"

Isis blew out her breath and collapsed into the dentist's chair, pushing her sweat-soaked curls off her forehead. She glanced at Marz, who was still waiting for an answer, and sat up. "We were just about to follow you into the Net when we got a call from Cyrus."

Marz's brows beetled. "And?"

"Harwood's awake!"

Marz went bolt upright in his swivel chair. "What?"

"Cyrus thought we should see for ourselves, but it didn't seem right for both of us to leave Lot 49, so I told Tech to go by himself, and that I'd keep watch on Justice. Anyway, I didn't detect anyone attempting to interfere with the thing—at least not from inside the club."

"You left the case? You walked out on a job?"

"That's your job, too, you know."

Marz glowered. "My job was to patrol the perimeter, which is exactly what I was doing."

The longer she stared at him, the softer her expression became. "I'm only saying that by the time I logged onto the Net, you were gone."

"I was incommunicado," Marz said. "Tell me about Mystery Notes."

"Tech finally called me to say that he'd spent

a couple of minutes talking to Harwood, and that Harwood seemed okay, even though his memory is sketchy. The doctor didn't want Tech hanging around, so he took off."

"Where's he now?"

"Probably on his way here. He and Cyrus were going to look for you in the Net." Isis narrowed her eyes at Marz. "So what's this about being incommunicado?"

Marz beckoned her over to the system's largest display screen, which was scrolling 0s and 1s like a pasta maker.

Isis shook her head back and forth. "Looks like garbled assembly code."

"Check out the string sequences. They're nothing like I've ever seen."

"Me, either. Very . . . elegant. Where'd you get it?"

"In the place where Bios7 got his shapeshifter."

Isis compressed her lips. "I thought you said you were tailing the neural net program—the space shuttle?"

Marz bristled. "I *was* tailing the space shuttle."

She stared at him. "And the shuttle led you to where Bios7 got the shapeshifter?"

Marz nodded. "Remember where he disappeared, close to the western end of the abyss? There's a portal there! It leads to a secret domain."

"Big deal, Einstein. There are tons of secret places in the Network."

"Not like this one. The place houses all kinds

of unbelievable constructs and craft. I had to upgrade my Terminator just to be allowed in."

"Why'd the space shuttle go there?"

"It went to a construct owned by guess who?— Mach Two. It spent about ten minutes uploading a slew of data packets, and the signatures of those packets are practically identical to the black file that flew out of Marty Morph." Marz's eyes were glowing, and practically screaming, he blurted out: "I think I've discovered Area X!"

"Calm down, Columbus." Isis placed her hand on his head. "Are you running a fever?"

He ignored the question. "When the space shuttle returned to the Net, it dropped off data packets at a dozen different megasites. But it brought most of them right back to CiscoSoft Entertainment and downloaded them into the neural net."

"I didn't pick up on that," Isis said.

"I know you didn't."

Isis folded her arms and glowered at him.

Marz called a map of the Network onscreen, highlighting the sites the space shuttle had visited on its return trip to CiscoSoft. Isis watched over his shoulder.

"I did some checking," Marz continued, "and each of these sites owns a Mach Two neural net. And we know that Mach Two is a front for Peerless Engineering."

Isis frowned. "All this means what, exactly?"

Marz folded his arms and sat back from the screen. "I think Peerless is using Mach Two to sell neural nets that have been programmed to report back to Peerless on the activities of the companies that buy them."

"Spysoft? That's what the space shuttle was picking up and delivering?"

"The spy programs could be Peerless' way of keeping tabs on the competition, and making sure it remains on top."

Isis' face wrinkled in uncertainty. "But why would Peerless insert spies into a neural net like Justice? What could Skander Bulkroad possibly hope to learn?"

Marz shrugged. "Marketing data, demographic information . . . Maybe he wants to scoop everyone about the *Cyberchallenge* finalists."

"No way. And why go to the trouble of creating a separate domain? Why not just install the spy programs directly into the neural nets to begin with?"

"Because the data gathered by the spies need to be delivered to Peerless in secret, and not by phone or computer."

Isis considered it. "So that's what was running wild inside Marty Morph—one of these data spies?"

"Maybe. Suppose one of Peerless' spies got loose and infected Marty's program. Maybe all that jumping around the Network was the spy's way of trying to find its way back to Area X."

Isis grinned in recollection. "Marty morphed into a white rabbit that kept saying, 'I'm late, I'm late.' "

Marz nodded. "Marty didn't just morph, he *shapeshifted*! And when we snagged him, the spysoft jumped because maybe it's programmed to detach the minute anyone detects it."

Isis took her lower lip between her teeth. "Marz, what if this Area X is the same domain Tech and Harwood found inside Peerless? The spy programs could have been what Tech and Harwood went up against. Scaum could have been, like the master spy, the head spook."

"If it is the same domain, then we've located a second entrance."

"Unless Peerless moved it."

"Moved it?" Marz said.

Isis looked at him. "They could do that, right?"

"I guess. Bios7 said that the domain was by invitation only, but I didn't have any trouble getting in."

"Could Peerless be doing selective emailing— actually inviting people to visit the domain?"

Marz massaged the back of his head. "It's pretty clear why Peerless would want to get a leg up on its corporate competitors. But I don't see why they'd invite someone like Bios7 into the domain."

"Maybe they're trying to put spy eyes into home cybersystems. Just like commercial sites that weasel into your processor and barrage you with pop-up adverts."

"Viral marketing," Marz said. "The domain rewards you with a new-generation cybercraft. But the next time you try logging into Grand

Adventure, you end up logging into Casino Land."

Isis shot him a worried look. "Marz, you said you had to upgrade the Terminator to get into the domain. That could mean that Data Discoveries has been infected."

Marz shook his head. "I made sure to purge all the downloads of any hidden attachments."

Isis' distress increased. "You found attachments?"

"A lot." Marz rubbed the back of his head.

"Not bad, Sherlock." Isis watched him. "What's wrong?"

"The back of my head feels kinda numb. It started just after I accepted the upgrade. But it's no big deal."

Isis began to pace in front of the console. "You should have waited for us at the portal, Marz."

He showed her a sheepish look. "Naw. I'm a pretty good pilot, too, you know."

Isis studied Marz and gave him a dazzling smile. "We better tell Tech."

"I tried hailing him just before you came in. He's not online."

Isis unclipped her cell phone from her belt and punched in Tech's number.

"*Ggraaa,*" she uttered a moment later, squeezing the small device as if she were wringing Tech's neck. "He's turned off his cell phone again!"

## Chapter 9

WEB WARRIORS

Tech squeezed his eyes shut against the white light pouring through his lids. Dreamy, he imagined himself in his Safehaven bedroom at sunrise, hoping for just a few more minutes of sleep before having to get up for school. When he blinked, though, it was as if the sun had gone nova.

And when he tried to shield his eyes, he discovered that his hands were tied behind his back.

His heart began to pound, and his breath came fast. Was he really bound, or was he trapped in the Network, *believing* he was bound? Could Scaum have caught up with him? Was his mind being devoured, as seemed to have happened last time?

But that couldn't be.

He remembered making a rushed but graceful-under-the-circumstances exit from the Network. Yes. He was in the medcenter lobby, his wireless wardrobe rig interfaced with Shady Grove's Network server, and he and Cyrus had been flying . . .

The puzzle began to reassemble itself.

They had been searching for Marz!

Then all at once they were trying to escape from a gang of outlaws, piloting a mishmash of craft. But with Cyrus' help he *had* escaped. Hurrying through the lobby for the revolving door . . . That was the last thing he remembered.

Little by little he allowed the light in, forcing himself finally to open his eyes.

Immediately he felt something wet and soft brush across his face, and he found himself nose to snout with a large golden retriever, sitting on its haunches and drooling happily. Behind the dog he could discern figures seated or moving about in the white glare. Then someone spoke.

"How you feeling, Tech?" It was a male voice, casually inquiring but tinged with malice. "We had to give you something to put you out. Couldn't risk causing a commotion at Shady Grove."

Tech swallowed. His throat was dry. When he managed to speak, his voice sounded weak and faraway. "Where am I?"

"Downtown."

"I'm hosting a locator implant," Tech said groggily.

Laughter.

"No you're not." A young woman's voice, from

the slightly smaller figure seated next to the man. "We scanned you. You're implant free."

"Who are you?" Tech asked. "Why are my hands tied?"

"Because my friends wouldn't condone spiking you with truth serum," the man said. "So instead we're going to do things the old-fashioned way. We'll ask questions and you'll provide answers. If we don't like what we hear, we'll be forced to make things uncomfortable for you."

His eyes beginning to adapt, Tech could make out at least six other people in the room, which—what with the way everyone's voices sounded—had to be large and high-ceilinged.

"I still say we'd be better off using electric pulse," someone said. "The stun gun's all warmed up."

"Why not just use a blade?" another said. "That's always worked in the past."

Despite his best efforts to remain calm, Tech began to sweat.

It was clear what had happened. Peerless had decided to make good on the warning they had delivered two weeks earlier. He had no clue why Bulkroad had chosen to act now, but obviously Peerless agents had been watching him, perhaps observed him flying with Cyrus, and had ultimately decided to kidnap him—in the real world.

"I'm not telling you Peerless scumballs anything," he said, putting as much force and anger into the words as he could muster.

The dog barked in agitation. Then the first

man rose from his chair and moved a couple of steps to the right, crossing in front of what Tech realized was a powerful spotlight, set atop a long table. When the man spoke again there was a change in his tone of voice. He sounded less certain, less threatening.

"What makes you think we work for Peerless?"

"You told me to not to interfere in your business, or have anything more to do with Cyrus. I guess you figure I haven't been listening."

Tech could hear hushed words being exchanged. Instantly he regretted his outburst. What if he had been picked up by Network Security? If so, he had already made things more difficult for himself by mentioning Peerless Engineering and Cyrus.

"You've got the wrong idea, Tech," the woman said.

Drawing a folding knife from a leather sheath she wore on her belt, she stood up and cut the ropes that bound Tech's hands. He rubbed his wrists, encouraging blood to circulate. The woman watched him.

"We're the ones who chased you and your gremlin friend out of the Network,"

Tech blinked in astonishment. "The pilots of those lame cyberships?"

"Lame?" someone said. "Who's this kid think he is?"

"A comedian," the first man said. "Why else would he choose a user name like *Tech*?"

A scattering of amused laughter. The dog barked pleasantly, and licked Tech's face again.

"Stop licking me! I give up—I'll tell you everything."

"Somebody switch off the spotlight," the woman said.

Tech's eyes took another long while to adjust. When they did, he saw that he had been correct about the room. It was a spacious loft, with huge skylights and floor-to-ceiling windows, all of which were draped and shaded. Six large optical cybersystems—complete with 3-D display screens and tandem flight chairs—hummed contentedly in the background.

As for Tech's abductors, they were as motley a group as the cybercraft they flew: good-looking and gawky, big-bellied and bearded, thin and tattooed. Some wore crooked hats and long interface coats, and others looked as if they had stepped from the virtual pages of *Hacker Magazine,* sporting long hair, baggy clothes, and circuit board accessories.

Tech recognized two of them as the floor polishers he had seen at Shady Grove.

"Definitely not Peerless or Syscops," Tech muttered suspiciously. "Who do you work for?"

"We don't 'work' for anyone," the group's apparent spokesperson said.

Tall, sinewy, and one of the tattooed few, his shaved head was decorated with intricate swirls of colored ink. Leather bracelets and a dozen necklaces gave him the look of a struggling rock star or actor.

"We know a friend of yours," the woman said. A green-eyed beauty, she had a heart-shaped face, luscious lips, and a bonnet of jet-black hair. "Harwood Strange."

Tech's mouth fell open. He glanced from one person to the next in dawning awareness. "You're Harwood's hacker allies!"

The woman smiled. "So Harwood told you about us."

Tech nodded, feeling more confident by the moment. "Everybody knows about you guys. You're the ones who wrote the Escarpment into the Network!"

The man's gray eyes bored into Tech's. "Then you should understand why we're not real pleased with your jumping it."

Confusion eroded Tech's confidence. "But it was Harwood who gave me the flight plan."

"We guessed that much," the woman said. "The question is, why did Harwood decide to go over to Peerless?"

Tech stared at her, his eyes narrowing. "Go over? Harwood *hates* Peerless. He gave me the flight plan as an escape route."

A bearded three-hundred-pounder seated behind the woman snorted a laugh. "You used too many knockout drops on the kid, Mackey. He's glitched."

Swaggering like a gunslinger, Mackey circled Tech then came to a halt in front of him. The golden retriever followed in Mackey's footsteps, bright-eyed and panting.

"Guy with the beard's Naif," Mackey said after a moment. He pointed to the young woman. "That's Chrome. I'll intro everyone else by and by."

Tech ruffled the dog's collarless neck. "Who's he?"

"Alladin."

Alladin barked and offered his right paw to Tech.

"Did I actually see him cyberflying, or am I glitched?"

Mackey smiled. "Best cyber-tracker we got."

"Wow, cool," Tech said. "But what do you want from me?"

Mackey pulled a chair opposite Tech's and straddled it. "We've been watching you ever since you made your jump."

Tech exhaled forcefully. "That's a relief. I thought I was just getting paranoid."

"Shut up and listen," Chrome said. "You've got every reason to be worried."

Mackey held Tech's gaze. "A couple of days before your jump, Harwood called us to ask if we'd done any tinkering with the abyss—anything that might affect the flight plan. His questions didn't arouse any suspicion, until he mentioned that he was planning on penetrating the Peerless Castle again. Then, the next thing we know, Harwood's in the hospital."

"And not two days later *you* jump the abyss," Chrome added, "assuring Skander Bulkroad once and for all that it can be bridged, and that the Wilds can be absorbed into the Network."

Mackey nodded. "You approached Harwood.

Either you're working for Peerless, and you somehow managed to get the flight program out of him, or Harwood cut a deal with Bulkroad, using you to feed Peerless information about the Escarpment."

Tech shook his head back and forth. "Wrong, wrong on all counts."

"Peerless has been hounding us for years," Chrome said. "That's why Strange was living like he was in Long Island. No friends, surrounded by all those cats. Broke and miserable, he finally caved."

Tech glowered at her. "You might have known him longer, but it's obvious I know him better. If Harwood was working for Peerless, how come he ended up in a coma?"

"Maybe Peerless double-crossed you," Mackey said. "After Peerless brought Harwood down, you thought you could go it alone. But Peerless sicced their security programs on you. That's when you jumped the abyss. Because you 'had to'—or you'd end up like Harwood."

"Don't try to con us, kid," big-bellied Naif said. "You were in it for the money. You could care less if Peerless takes over the Wilds."

Tech kept shaking his head.

"You're going to deny working for Peerless," Chrome said, "when that blue gremlin you were flying with has Peerless software written all over it?"

Tech looked up at her and laughed. "Yeah, but that's because the gremlin originally came from Peerless."

"So you admit it," Mackey said. "Who's the gremlin's pilot—or is it just a program?"

"Well, it is and it isn't."

"Meaning what?"

"The gremlin's Cyrus Bulkroad."

"Skander's son?" Chrome asked in bewildered surprise.

"Skander Bulkroad's *AI*," Tech said.

"Now I can't find Cyrus or Tech," Isis said in exasperation.

Reclined in the newer of the interface chairs, she had gone into the Network to search for them after failing to reach Tech by cell phone. Her hands tweaked the joystick and her feet worked the control pedals.

"Where's The Prowler? Where'd you put it?"

"Bay door three. I did some mod fixes."

The skiff had never looked better. She swiveled the chair around to face Marz. "Thanks, Marz."

Marz blushed. He was still seated at the cybersystem, toying with the mystifying codes he had uploaded from Mach Two's site in the hidden domain. "No wonder Bios7's shapeshifter was so amazing. But I think I can work with this. I can definitely make something of this."

"Marz!" Isis said. "Did you hear what I said? I can't locate either of them."

He made a face at her. "Stop worrying. They'll check in. While you're in the Net, check in on *Cyberchallenge* for me."

"Oh, you mean like do everyone's job again?"

"Yeah. A friend of mine's one of the contestants."

"I know, I saw him."

"So cruise on over there."

Isis scowled at him. "Yes, sir." She saluted, then tasked her eyephones to go Network-active and maneuvered The Prowler to CiscoSoft Entertainment's megasite. Shortly, Marz heard her make a surprised sound.

"What's up?"

Isis slid the eyephones up onto her freckled forehead. "Ramlock was the first one voted out."

Marz's eyebrows beetled. "That can't be. His Hummer was capable of handling any cyber-environment *Cyberchallenge* could design."

"It wasn't because his craft failed. He got tossed for using illegal soft. He cheated."

"No way," Marz said. "He was voted most-valuable player in our school. He'd never cheat."

"Well, then it was somebody else named Ramlock who looks just like him."

"Marz, Isis," Cyrus said suddenly from the office speakers.

Both of them turned to the mirrored wall that concealed Cyrus' hardware trappings. Clearly the AI wasn't in the Network anymore, but his voice sounded worried.

"What's wrong, Cyrus?" Isis asked. "Is it Harwood?"

"No, Isis. It's Tech."

The blue gremlin appeared onscreen in the flight room.

"Marz, shortly after Tech's meeting with Harwood, he and I began searching for you in the Network. We had traced you to the western terminus of the Escarpment when we were set upon by a gang of outlaws who flew from the Wilds."

"Outlaws?"

"I wasn't able to identify their craft by signatures," Cyrus continued. "They pursued us, firing disabling code, as if trying to drive us away. I conveyed Tech to an emergency egress, and he made a graceful exit from the Network. I returned to the Escarpment to search for evidence of where our assailants might have headed, but they covered their tracks. Then I re-entered Shady Grove's cybersystem and accessed the real-time security cameras trained on the lobby. But Tech was nowhere in sight."

"Then he's probably on his way here," Marz said. "He just has his interface rig and phone turned off."

"No."

Isis' troubled look deepened.

"When I couldn't find him," Cyrus said, "I accessed the camera recordings themselves and discovered something most disconcerting. Tech was taken—abducted by three men."

Isis raised her head, eyes blazing. "Oh, no."

"NetSec agents?" Marz asked, leaping to his feet. "Syscops?"

"They were disguised as hospital workers," Cyrus said. "I managed to infiltrate the municipal security cameras, and saw the men transfer Tech to a van and drive off. The van's license plate, which is expired, does not correspond to the vehicle description. I ran likenesses of the men through a face-recognition program, but found no matches."

"Have you contacted Felix?" Isis said.

"He's on his way."

"Who would want to snatch Tech?" Marz said, pacing in circles.

Isis watched him for a moment, then positioned herself for the AI's video pickups. "Cyrus, what are you leaving out?"

"I didn't want to withhold anything," Cyrus said in distress. "But it doesn't seem my place to reveal what Tech told me!"

"Cough up those bytes," Isis said. *"Now!"*

"Two days ago, Tech confessed to me that shortly following my reassembly he received a message from unidentified parties, warning him to desist in having any further contact with *me.*"

Isis firmed her lips in anger. "Oh, great."

"Cyrus, who are these unidentified parties?" Marz asked.

Cyrus took a long moment to respond. "I have no proof, Marz, but it stands to reason that the threat could have come only from Peerless Engineering."

WEB WARRIORS

Chrome brought Tech some crackers and soda, and he took a long slug from the can. Alladin was sitting on his haunches alongside Tech, tongue unfurled, and panting. Tech set the can down and wiped his mouth with the back of his right hand. Alladin made as if to lick Tech's right hand, only to snatch the crackers from his left.

"Smart dog."

Chrome nodded. "You have no idea."

Mackey was seated opposite Tech, still shaking his head in wonder at Tech's revelation about Cyrus. "All those years we thought Cyrus was dead," he said. "And now you tell us that we were searching for an artificial intelligence the whole time."

"Where is Cyrus now?" Chrome asked, not entirely successful at making it sound like a casual question.

"I haven't a clue," Tech said.

"But you were flying with him when we found you."

Tech shrugged. "He comes and goes."

Chrome and Mackey traded glances. "Earlier you said something about Peerless warning you not to have anything more to do with Cyrus."

Tech fumbled for an explanation. "Yeah, well, that's because I think Peerless thought Cyrus was the one who gave me the flight plan for jumping the abyss."

"Why would Cyrus know the flight plan?" Chrome asked. "Even we don't know it."

Tech gaped at her and Mackey. "How can you not know it? Harwood and you guys *created* the Escarpment."

Chrome smiled ruefully. "Yes, and to protect it, each of us memorized only certain of the code sequences that support it. Acting together, we can do pretty much what we want with the Escarpment—we have contingency plans that can be executed at a moment's notice—but the flight plan was Harwood's piece of the puzzle, and his alone."

Naif trundled over to Tech. "If what you've told us is true, then you're in serious danger, kid. Peerless won't stop at anything to get that flight plan."

Tech gazed at the floor, then lifted to his head. "Then I'm not the only one in danger."

"Someone else knows the flight plan?" Mackey said.

Tech glanced at him. "I'm talking about Harwood."

Mackey snorted. "Harwood's only in danger if he wakes up."

Tech stared them down. "He is awake."

Chrome's eyes widened. "What? When?"

"Today. That's why I was at Shady Grove. Because this Dr. Matterling revived Harwood."

"Revived him how?" Mackey asked.

"By bringing Harwood back into the Network."

"This doesn't sound good," Chrome said.

Naif nodded. "We wondered why Matterling was at Shady Grove."

"You know him?" Tech asked.

"We've been keeping an eye on Harwood, too," Mackey explained.

"The guy you know as Matterling is actually a Peerless technopath named Agrew," Naif added. "He's one of Bulkroad's top people."

Tech shook his head. "That can't be. His credentials checked out."

Naif laughed without merriment. "Of course, they checked out. Peerless ain't sloppy, boy."

"Did you talk to Harwood?" Chrome asked Tech.

"For a couple of minutes. His memory was foggy."

"Foggy how?" Mackey said.

"Well, like it took him a minute to remember his cats."

Alladin barked at mention of the cats, and

Chrome patted him on the head. "Harwood would never forget those cats," she said. "He lived for those animals."

"But I'll bet 'Matterling' had an explanation for the memory lapse," Naif said.

Tech nodded. "He said it was common in recently revived patients."

"Stop for a minute," Chrome said, holding out her arms. "Why would Peerless send Agrew to revive Harwood when, after all these years, they finally had Harwood where they wanted him—in a coma?"

"For the flight plan," Naif said. "Like Tech says, only he and Harwood know it."

"No!" Tech said suddenly, shooting to his feet. "There's someone else!"

"Who?" Mackey asked.

Tech's looked at him wide-eyed. "We've got to get to Data Discoveries before it's too late!"


"Marz, I'm really worried," Isis said. "I think we should call the police."

"And tell them what? Peerless Engineering kidnapped Tech? Think about it. All we've got is the hunch of an AI no one is even supposed to know about." Marz shook his head. "I say we raid the Peerless Castle for information. Maybe we can match the faces of the kidnappers to the names of people on Peerless' payroll."

Isis gnawed at her forefinger. "Felix would go ballistic." She slouched into Felix's swivel chair, closing her eyes and shaking her head back and forth.

Marz had his mouth open to say something, when Aqua Brockton knocked on the office door and eased inside.

"There are two scary guys here to see you, Marz," Aqua said.

Marz glanced at the video monitor that showed the waiting room, where two men in baggy gray suits were standing by the front door. When the taller of the pair turned toward the wide-angle camera, Marz saw the man's thinning hair, wire-rimmed glasses, and long white beard.

"Mystery Notes!"

Isis whirled to face the monitor. "What? Are you sure?"

Marz pointed at the screen. "See for yourself. And the guy with him is Dr. Matterling."

"I can't believe it," Isis said, flushed with excitement. "Aqua, tell them to come in."

Aqua left the room, and Marz pressed the button on Felix's desk that sealed the mirrored wall.

Isis showed him a puzzled look. "Why are you closing Cyrus off?"

"We don't know if Tech told Mystery Notes about Cyrus being an AI. It might be too much of a shock for him."

Isis grinned. "No wonder you get the big bucks." Then she grew serious. "Marz, should we tell Harwood about Tech?"

He considered it briefly. "Let's just play it by ear."

Isis nodded and swung toward the office door, patting her curls into some semblance of order.

"I'm so freaked. I only met him once, but it feels like I've known him forever."

"Yeah. It's like he's been away on a long trip, not in a coma." Marz looked around the room. "I wonder if he'll like all the new cyberware?"

"He's bound to."

Harwood Strange and Dr. Matterling came through the door.

Marz and Isis stood staring at Strange for a long moment, then launched themselves across the room and hugged him around the waist. When he didn't so much as pat them on the shoulders, they stepped back in embarrassment.

"We're so glad to see you, Harwood," Isis said at last.

Harwood gazed at her without reply, then looked at Marz. "Marz," he said, drawing out the word.

Marz swallowed audibly, nodded, and gestured to Isis. "Remember Isis, Mys—er, Harwood?"

Harwood's flaring eyebrows met in the center of his forehead.

"Isis Whitehawk?" she supplied. "We were together at The Hackers Outlet? My father's a big fan of yours?"

"Your father?"

Isis frowned. "Merlin Whitehawk?"

"Isis saved our butts from a couple of Decepts," Marz added.

"Truly?" Harwood said. "Then I'm even more sorry I don't remember her."

Isis mustered a smile. "That's okay. Tech said

that you'd, um, misplaced some of your memories."

Harwood's hooded gaze took in the room. "Where is Tech?"

Marz and Isis exchanged brief glances. "He's out on company business," Marz said.

"We didn't expect you to leave the medcenter so soon," Isis said, desperate to change the subject.

Matterling responded to it. "Mr. Strange is making good progress. I felt we might be able to jog his memory by visiting familiar places."

Harwood continued to glance around the room.

Marz blew out his breath. "Actually, Mystery, we think that Tech might have been kidnapped by agents of Peerless Engineering."

Harwood tipped his head to one side in surprise. "What leads you to that conclusion?"

"Well, for one thing," Isis began, "Peerless warned him to stay away from Cyrus." She stopped herself.

"Tech told you about Cyrus?" Marz asked carefully.

"Yes. He said that Cyrus was doing well."

"Anything else?"

Harwood smiled without showing his teeth. "You mean, about not recognizing him as the Cyrus I once knew?"

Isis exhaled in relief. "Exactly. We just didn't want to spring it on you."

Harwood stared at her. "So you believe that Peerless abducted Tech because of his ongoing relationship with Cyrus?"

"We don't know what else to think," Marz said. "Unless it's because of what you and Tech discovered inside the castle."

"The domain."

Isis nodded. "And Scaum."

"Scaum, yes . . ." Harwood said. "And what does Cyrus think of all this?"

"Ask him yourself," Marz said, smiling mischievously.

"How might I do that? I don't how to contact him."

"He's right here," Isis said, motioning to the mirrored wall.

Harwood pivoted slightly and stared at his own reflection. "I don't understand."

Marz moved to Felix's desk and activated the sliding mirrors. In a moment, Cyrus' score of data storage towers were revealed, along with the screen that displayed the AI's self-selected countenance. Harwood stepped rigidly to the transparent wall of the air-conditioned space and pressed his hands to the glass, as if trying to touch Cyrus.

"So this is where you reside," he said almost to himself. "Very cozy."

As program gremlin, Cyrus appeared on screen. "Hello, Mystery Notes. It has been a long time."

"Too long," Harwood said, running his eyes over the towers and thick cables that linked them.

"We finally meet face-to-face. There's so much

to discuss." The gremlin smiled. "You'll visit with me through the Network?"

"Yes."

Cyrus called a series of numbers to the screen. "This is a code that will take you inside Data Discoveries' construct in the Wilds."

Harwood read the code aloud, clearly committing it to memory. "I'll be visiting you soon, Cyrus. You can count on it."

## Chapter 11

**WEB WARRIORS**

Isis and Marz were still discussing Harwood Strange's surprise visit when a sudden disturbance in the waiting room drew their attention to the monitor affixed to the wall. By the time they turned to the screen, however, whoever or whatever had caused the turmoil had passed beyond Aqua's desk and was apparently headed for the office.

No sooner had Marz leaped from Felix's swivel chair than Tech came through the office door, followed by Aqua Brockton, a shave-skulled guy of about thirty, and a frisky golden retriever.

"Tech!" Marz and Isis said in stunned disbelief.

"Aqua, lock the office," Tech said breathlessly. "Don't let anyone in."

Aqua looked to Marz for confirmation. "Totally?"

Marz glanced at his brother, then nodded to Aqua. "Do like Tech says."

Tech folded himself into one of the armchairs, while Marz and Isis glanced from him to Mackey to Alladin, and back to Tech.

Tech motioned to his companions. "This is Mackey. That's Alladin. Mackey, that's Isis, and that's my brother, Marz."

"Good to meet both of you," Mackey said.

Alladin barked enthusiastically.

Marz and Isis continued to shift their gazes back and forth.

"Did Mackey help you escape?" Isis asked at last.

Tech regarded at her in bewilderment. "Escape from what?"

"From Peerless," Isis practically shrieked. "Cyrus saw you get grabbed at the medcenter. We thought . . ."

Tech was nodding, and chuckling to himself. "Actually, Mackey's the one who grabbed me."

Isis' gaze hardened. She jumped up, threatening Mackey with a broken joystick. "Don't move, you!"

"No, no, it's okay," Tech said, erupting from the chair. "Mackey's an old friend of Harwood's. He just wanted to, uh, talk to me about my jumping the abyss."

Isis kept her scowl in place. "By throwing you into the back of an unregistered van?" She focused her fury on Mackey. "What happened to just IM-ing, *Mackey*?"

"We were only trying to scare him." He glanced at Tech and smiled. "And let me tell you, Tech doesn't scare easily."

While Isis and Marz were trying to digest everything, Alladin hopped up into the dentist's chair, nuzzled one of the interface sets over his head, and started to bark.

"What's with your dog, man?" Marz asked.

Mackey went over to Alladin and scratched him behind the ears. "He's fond of flying."

"He *flies*?" Marz and Isis said at the same time.

Mackey nodded. "He's even got his own craft."

Isis shook her head, as if to clear it. "Guess that's easier than walking him, huh?"

Mackey laughed shortly. "You guys only funny here, or do you take your act on the road?"

Isis folded her arms over her chest. "You've got a cyberflying dog and *I'm* the one who has a road act?"

Tech frowned at her. "Hey, take it easy, will you."

She turned to him and straightened her shoulders. "I'm so glad you're back." He had almost completed a smile when she added: " 'CAUSE NOW I CAN START HATING YOU!"

"Whoa," Tech said, backing away.

She pursued him, jabbing her forefinger in his chest. "Let's start with not telling us about the warning you received from Peerless, you jerk!"

Tech blinked. "Who told—Cyrus!" he yelled to the room.

"Don't even think about blaming Cyrus," Isis

went on. "He was only trying to help us figure out who snatched you."

Tech adopted a contrite look. "I didn't say anything about the warning because I didn't want to upset you."

"Upset us," Isis said. "You think you're in this alone, hot shot?"

Mackey laughed again, and clapped Tech on the shoulder. "Redheads."

"Tell me about it," Tech said out of the corner of his mouth.

Isis glowered at the two of them.

Marz shot Tech a look. "What the heck's going on, bro?"

"It's about Mystery Notes, and the flight plan," Tech started to say.

"You just missed him," Marz said.

Tech snapped to. "He called?"

"No, he stopped by."

Tech stared openmouthed at his brother for a long moment. "He was here—Harwood came *here*?"

"Chill, Tech," Isis said. "Dr. Matterling was with him. They're visiting places Harwood was on the day he faded, hoping to jumpstart his memory."

Tech tried to speak, but couldn't; so Mackey spoke for him.

"Matterling's a phony. His real name is Agrew, and he works for Peerless. He may have revived Harwood, but we're not sure why."

Tech swung to Marz. "Did Harwood say anything about the new deck and flight chair?"

Marz's brow furrowed. "He didn't even mention them, but—"

"Did he remember the cats?"

"We didn't talk about the cats," Isis said.

Marz frowned. "He didn't remember Isis."

"Did he say anything about Cyrus?" Mackey asked.

Isis glanced at Marz, then bit her lower lip. "They talked."

Tech's face fell, then he suddenly perked up. "He must have been shocked to learn that Cyrus is an AI, right?"

"Not really," Isis said quietly.

Tech waited for more.

"I mean, we figured you'd already told him about Cyrus," Marz added.

Tech shook his head. "I didn't tell him, I didn't say that Cyrus was an AI."

Marz watched his brother. "I don't get it, Tech. Then how did Mystery Notes know?"

"Marz, open Cyrus' room," Tech said quickly.

Mackey smiled in surprise as the mirrored wall parted.

Tech went directly to the microphone below Cyrus' screen, and hailed him, but the gremlin didn't appear. Marz returned to the cybersystem and did rapid input at the keyboard. His face was ashen when he looked up.

"Cyrus is gone."

"Try hailing him again," Isis started to say, when the videophone chirped.

Tech threw himself into Felix's chair and hit the receive button. Positioning himself for the phone camera, he waited for the screen to display the caller, but the small display remained blank.

Then Cyrus' voice issued from the speaker.

"Tech, I'm relieved to see you back at Data Discoveries," he began in an excited tone. "I actually spoke with Mystery Notes! He's here, he's here."

"No," Tech interrupted. "It's a trap! Get out of the octagon."

Without warning, the optical processors that oversaw Cyrus' memory towers let out a prolonged electronic shriek. Isis and Marz put their hands to their ears to shut out the sound, and Alladin howled from the dentist's chair.

"Cyrus!" Tech yelled toward the videophone's microphone. "Cyrus!"

Mackey's handsome face warped into a mask of bitterness.

"Peerless got to him."

Skander Bulkroad moved with determined strides through the castle's northwest upper-tier corridor. The low heels of his leather boots left scant impressions in a narrow carpet that depicted unicorns and other Renaissance-era mythical beasts, all meticulously recreated by Peruvian weavers.

What had once been an open-air walkway linking the castle's north and west turrets had been walled in and roofed over as a workspace for Peerless' cadre of Network-support specialists—the company's cybervassals. To both sides of Bulkroad sat rank after rank of cyberengineers, doing nimble input at keyboards and a wide array of other devices that kept the Network running smoothly. It would have been easy enough to replace the workers with machines—many of them were already outfitted with wireless interface receivers—but Bulkroad felt that the engineers afforded the Network a kind of handwritten naturalness. Perfect at the core but frayed at the edges, Bulkroad's Network was like the carpet that graced the marble floor, whose deliberate defects attested to the innate imperfection of the universe.

He wore a long-sleeved tunic gathered by a girdle, with a short capelike mantle fastened by an elaborately carved golden clasp. A soft cap covered his bald head, and natural fiber stockings sheathed his thick calves. Both of his ears held audio beads, whose antennae resembled earrings, and a tiny self-adhering microphone sat at the right corner of his mouth, like a beauty mark. As he walked, basking in the persistent purring of the machines, he conversed continuously with his aides and assistants elsewhere in the castle, and in some cases elsewhere in the world—and off it, as well.

Bulkroad entered the castle's north turret simultaneously with the arrival of his personal elevator, which greeted him with a chime, and swung open. Stepping inside, he pressed the down button, and the glass cylinder began a slow descent.

Below and to all sides of him spread the Virtual Network.

He was like a deity, deigning to descend from his heavenly abode to regard his creation.

But, in fact, Bulkroad remained very much in the real world, for the cyberspace that filled the north tower from top to bottom was merely a holographic representation of the virtual world, with its lower, middle, and upper levels, its data highways and pedestrian malls, its geometrically shaped corporate headquarters, storage facilities, theme parks, and amusement rides.

As one of the chief architects of the Network, Bulkroad had insisted on having a model upon which he could gaze, to monitor his creation in real time, tweak the dimensions of a construct here, extend a thoroughfare there, render adjustments in accordance with the grand design of his vision. Maps of the sort that came stock with every cybersystem simply didn't do justice to that vision. The Network had to be seen like this to be appreciated for what it was: not merely a work in progress, but a work of art.

At each level, Bulkroad had the option of moving the elevator car horizontally through the hologram to bring him closer to clusters of constructs or streams of ceaselessly moving cybercraft— pods, fantasy animals, saucers, and the rest—but he didn't choose to exercise that option. Instead, as the car continued to drop through the administrative levels toward the virtual castle that bore the company name, he turned in place to behold the vast panoramas. Ultimately, and with unmitigated disgust, he swiveled to face the horrid flaw that broke the symmetry of his vision: the open wound that was the Escarpment and the abyss beyond.

But just then an event was taking place that would bring him one step closer to healing that wound, and enable him to expand the Network to the south, completing the project Bulkroad and most of his uncommon partners had agreed on almost fifteen years earlier, when his eyes had been opened to the greater truths of the universe.

He gazed across the abyss at the octagon Cyrus had raised in the heart of the Wilds. Bulkroad had loathed having had to add the construct to the holographic reproduction, but there was no denying the octagon's existence, and everything that existed in the Network had to be represented. Even so, he had insisted at the time that the octagon be marked temporary.

Bulkroad had just launched the elevator car out over the abyss—something he was capable of doing only in this ersatz Network—when a wheezing voice spoke in his right ear.

"The offensive is under way."

Bulkroad smiled. "I promised that the Wilds would be yours, Scaum. It's just a matter of time now."

"What are your plans for Cyrus?"

"Once the virus takes hold, we should have no trouble gaining full access to the octagon, and downloading Cyrus to machines specifically designed to receive and contain him. The shielded storage modules that house Cyrus at Data Discoveries will be hopelessly corrupted. When Cyrus' transfer is completed, we will delete the files stored in the Data Discoveries. Once we possess him, we'll issue our ultimatum to Data Discoveries that they surrender the flight plan for the abyss or see their precious AI destroyed."

"You're so certain that they will surrender the flight plan?"

"I know human beings, Scaum. After what Tech and the others have already risked for Cyrus—yes, I am that certain that they will surrender the flight plan."

"I would have gone after the younger brother."

Bulkroad sniggered. "We can always do that if necessary. By taking Cyrus, we complete two goals with one move."

"After the flight plan is received, you'll return Cyrus to them?"

"For a time, yes. But Cyrus won't be the AI they have come to know. He'll be working for us, as was always meant to be the case." Bulkroad paused briefly. "But I want a little time with Cyrus first. I want Cyrus to understand the damage he has done. I want him to hear from me what his punishment will be."

Bulkroad regarded the octagon, which was already beginning to deteriorate. "The cyberpoison appears to be working. I fear that Tech and his allies won't stand idly by, but I leave them to you, Scaum. I suggest you make use of

some of the sorry cyberfliers you have commandeered, if only to distance Peerless from suspicion."

"Is it wise to reveal my conscripts so soon?"

"In the Wilds, they will scarcely attract notice."

"Then I myself will command them—in atone-
ment for allowing events to come to this."

Bulkroad smiled to himself. "You're still relatively new to this world, and there is much to
learn."

Scaum didn't argue the point. "In humans, un-
predictability becomes a formidable weapon.
It's no wonder you have managed to rid this
planet of any would-be competitors. Your
species is to be applauded—if only in its final
hour."

WEB WARRIORS

Tech snugged the control pedal restraints around his pristine cross-trainers and swiveled the dentist's chair in the direction of the office. Through the open door he could see warning telltales flashing on several of Cyrus' storage towers. Isis was on the far side of the plate glass that partitioned the AI's room, doing her best to control electrical fires that had erupted from two of control console's access panels. Tech caught a fleeting glimpse of her—a dust-mask covering her nose and mouth and a small fire-extinguisher gripped in her gloved hands—before he swung the chair to face the flight room cybersystem.

"We've got widespread firewall failures throughout the octagon," Marz was saying, his eyes riveted to data that filled one of the monitor screens. "Backup shields are going active now, but they won't hold for long."

"Is Peerless using a virus?"

"Yeah, but nothing I can counter with the usual antivirals. This one's system specific." Marz paused his input long enough to show Tech a fearful look. "They're targeting Cyrus' assembly codes."

An attack only Peerless could launch, Tech told himself. Bulkroad, who already knew Cyrus' weak points, had needed only a way to get to the AI, and now Harwood Strange had provided him with a direct route.

Tech shut his eyes behind the wraparound interface visor, sick at heart for what Peerless had done to Harwood to cause him to betray Cyrus. Although the reason for their contemptible act was obvious. Peerless couldn't take the chance that Cyrus would get the rest of his memories back and blow the lid off whatever depraved scheme Skander Bulkroad's corporation was running.

For the whole trip between Mackey's loft and Data Discoveries, Tech had been worried that Marz was the one who had been targeted by Peerless, when all the while it had been Cyrus.

Tech recalled Mackey's frown of hopelessness as he had hurried from the office, fearful that Peerless had also wrested the abyss flight plan from Harwood, and that the attack on Cyrus' octagon might be a prelude to an all-out attack on the Wilds.

He glanced through the office door once more. Noise crazed the screen that was Cyrus' display.

Even when the screen cleared intermittently, there was no sign of the gremlin—only a white-out of electronic snow.

Tech vised his hands on the joystick. "Marz, prep the V-7."

"Locked and loaded. You taking the shortcut to the Wilds?"

Tech shook his head. "I can't risk jumping the abyss—not now. I'll go over the west end of the Escarpment."

Marz's face lit up. "Tech, there's something important I've gotta tell you about that western route."

"Important how?"

"You were right about there being a gateway there. I went through it."

Tech stared at him in bafflement. "You what?"

"Not now, bro, you need to fly."

Just then, Isis emerged from Cyrus' room. She glanced at Marz's crowded screens. "Stay here and help Marz," Tech said. Isis looked to Marz for an okay.

Marz nodded at her.

Tech reclined the dentist's chair and went virtual.

No sooner had the grid resolved beneath him than he rocketed for the abyss. Designed to be quick and lethal, the fighter jet roared south—paralleling the Ribbon, though one level above it. Tech called up data displays of the software programs Marz had imported, which ran the gamut from high-density armor to codebreaker weaponry.

In minutes the Blackout was streaking over the shallow western terminus of the abyss. As fixated as he was on reaching the octagon, Tech couldn't resist gazing around, wondering about the location of the gate Marz had apparently found, and just what lay beyond it.

Shortly, the octagon came into view in the distance. But even this far from the construct Tech gained some sense of the power Peerless was bringing to bear against Cyrus. The Blackout began to lose speed, and the software programs grew sluggish and unresponsive. It was as if the craft had entered a potent magnetic field.

Tech banked to the east, adhering to a course that kept the Blackout at the periphery of the maelstrom. He was due north of the octagon when the backup shields went active. Rising from the construct's base, diamond-shaped ruby-red scales began to march up the sides of the octagon.

But Tech could see why Marz had been so sullen.

Directly above the eight-sided construct hovered an enormous cylindrical airship, modeled after the zeppelins and dirigibles of old, except that this one was raining death on the octagon, in the form of a torrent of virused droplets, fired from weapons turrets and a whiskerlike array of forward batteries. The droplets fell like pebbles into water, each stirring a virulent ripple in the octagon's ruddy sheathing, then spreading outward in code-gobbling concentric rings, which began to corrode the shield like acid rain.

The Data Discoveries sign that crowned the octagon was the first to go, winking out and disappearing.

There was no time to waste. Sending the control pedals to the floor, Tech powered the Blackout into the heart of the storm, his fingers dancing over the joystick buttons to launch packets of disabling code against the deadly zeppelin. Ascending to avoid return fire, he climbed over the curved top of the virtual airship, loosing clusters of data bombs and codebusters.

All to no effect.

"Marz, I'm throwing everything I've got against this blimp, and it isn't even vexed. It's zeroing the octagon with virus."

"Get clear, Tech. I'm putting something together that could buy Cyrus some time."

"Roger, that. I'm outward bound," Tech said, pulling the joystick toward him and soaring high above the Wilds.

Far below, a shaft began to rise from the center of the octagon. Just short of the blimp, the leading end of the shaft blossomed into an immunity umbrella, deflecting the virus rain into the gullies and canyons that fractured the surrounding cyberterrain.

"Yeah!" Tech said, raising his right fist in victory.

"Don't celebrate yet," Marz said. "Peerless is already mutating the virus. It'll eat through the umbrella soon enough, and we'll be right back where we started."

Tech made a low pass over the dirigible. The shower was becoming more vigorous. Soon the virus was gushing from wide-mouthed dispenser ports in the blimp's belly.

"Marz, do you have a fix on who's controlling the blimp?"

"I'm working on it. But the attack is being routed through hundreds of different sites."

"Can we move Cyrus out of the octagon?"

"There isn't time."

"What about severing his connections to the Network?"

"Impossible. Too much of him still resides in the Net. Severing the connections would crash everything."

Isis broke into the conversation. "Look sharp! Hostile craft approaching from the north."

Tech took the Blackout through a broad one-eighty and activated his forward scanners. Seconds later, when craft profiles had begun to take shape in one of the visor's data windows, he gasped in surprise. Some of the craft looked as if they had surfaced from the deepest depths of oceanic trenches; others might have escaped from a museum display of medieval weapons.

"I'm getting a visual on the craft," Tech said, "but I don't believe what I'm seeing." An even more astounding sight—for its unexpectedness—left him briefly silent. "Bios7's shapeshifter is flying with them! What's he doing here?"

"It is the shapeshifter, and it isn't," Marz said a moment later. "The shapeshifter's hosting some kind of attachment. Its signature is a variation of the signature I picked up from Marty Morph, and later from CiscoSoft's neural net."

Tech couldn't make sense of what Marz was telling him, but he knew better than to hang around the octagon any longer. Releasing the last of the Blackout's data bombs, he accelerated away from the construct, out over the Wilds in the direction of the mountainous Uplift region.

Behind him, the squadron of bizarre craft had formed up around the defense umbrella Marz had deployed, and were already eating through it. Punching through the shield, a vanguard of driller craft began to cyclone down the shaft toward the vulnerable core of the octagon.

Tech's gaze lingered on one of the craft. "Marz, who'd you say built the tricked out Hummer you saw at Ziggy's Cyberchop?"

"Ramlock," Marz said.

"As in *Cyberchallenge* Ramlock?" Tech said in shock. "Travis?"

"Yeah, why, Tech?"

" 'Cause it looks to me like Ramlock is Bios7's wingman!"

Isis watched Marz enter rapid commands into two separate keyboards. Mind-boggling aggregates of code appeared on the data displays, only to be replaced by equally extraordinary combinations. In Cyrus' room, one storage tower after another fell eerily silent, as Cyrus began to lose consciousness.

Marz began to mutter as he typed.

"Some of the craft match the signatures of ones the space shuttle delivered from the domain to CiscoSoft. And suddenly Peerless is deploying them against the octagon."

Isis stared at the screens in mounting bewilderment. "You didn't say they were craft. You said they were spy programs."

"They are. Peerless isn't just infiltrating the programs into neural nets. It's infiltrating them into *cybercraft*." Marz leaned back from one of the monitors in order to give Isis a better look at the screen. "Ramlock's Hummer isn't the only one. Every craft that's been disqualified from *Cyberchallenge* is now being used to attack Cyrus."

"But Bios7 was never a contestant. How could Peerless get hold of his shapeshifter?"

"Because Bios7 got the shapeshifter in the domain—just the way I got my Terminator upgraded to a Mace."

Isis gawked at him. "Marz, *you* were in the domain."

Marz cut her off with a shake of his head. "I told you, I purged the downloads of any masked attachments. Besides, Bios7's shapeshifter had a slightly different signature when we first followed it, which could mean that a craft can only be taken over after multiple visits to the domain."

"But Peerless has *fleets* of cybercraft. Why would it need Bios7's, or Ramlock's, or anybody else's?"

"I don't know—yet. But I do know where the blimp is being controlled from." Marz moved his headset microphone closer to his mouth. "Tech, are you there?"

"Grazing the Uplift, bro."

"The blimp's being remotely controlled from Mach Two's site—on the far side of the hidden gate I told you about. It's Area X."

"All right! How do I get in?"

Marz smiled lightly. "I'm opening the garage again. I've got a surprise for you."

**WEB WARRIORS**

Boring through the second *o* in the cybercondo advertisement, Tech found himself in a gray netherworld that made even the virtual network seem a *real* place by comparison.

*Area X.*

Thickening into a web of braided tendrils, the fog held him fast.

He loosened his grip on the joystick and waited, taking a moment to appraise the new-generation cybercraft Marz had built. Marz said that it had begun its life as a spined sphere, resembling a medieval weapon. Now, though, it sported paired turbothrusters, maneuvering vanes, armaments, and a host of other enhancements Marz had downloaded from Mach Two's construct in the hidden domain.

A text message appeared in Tech's headset visor.

*Welcome back. A further upgrade*

*for your Mace is available. Do you wish to upgrade now or later?*

*Later*, Tech answered, using his joystick to click on the appropriate box.

As Marz had explained it—briefly, at any rate—upgrading was exactly what Peerless wanted visitors to do, because with each upgrade came attachments that would eventually place a visitor's craft under Peerless' control.

Peerless was using Area X as a means of moving super-smart spy programs into the Network. Once installed in the neural nets of various Network sites, the clandestine programs not only served as moles—keeping Peerless informed about the activities of its multinational competitors—but also as virtual operatives, capable of executing directives issued by Peerless. Bios7's shapeshifter, Ramlock's Hummer, and the craft of several other *Cyberchallenge* contestants had already been seized by the spy programs, and were being employed in the assault on the octagon.

Marz was at a loss to explain Peerless' aim in commandeering the craft, but to Tech the strategy made perfect sense. By usurping the craft of cyberjocks and frequent fliers, Peerless' sinister programs were free to zip about the Network without arousing suspicion—to hide in plain sight, just as Cyrus had been doing when disguised as a program gremlin.

But Cyrus' disguise hadn't kept him safe. Only moments earlier, Marz had told Tech that some of the machines that supported Cyrus in

Data Discoveries had been corrupted by Peerless' virus, and that the AI was in real danger of being recaptured by his creator, Skander Bulkroad.

Given the go-to by the domain gate, Tech piloted the modified Mace forward, further removing himself from communication with Data Discoveries, and emerging from the pervasive fog into a confined but dizzying space of uncompleted constructs. Frameworks and structural supports gave the constructs the same medieval look as the structures he and Harwood had seen in the Peerless domain.

They were one and the same.

The realization stunned him momentarily. Sky and ground had been altered, and the jagged peaks that had risen like dragon's teeth from whirlpooling mist had been given exotic labels and addresses, but there was no camouflaging the disquieting *realness* of the place.

But what had prompted Peerless to move the domain? Or was the cybercondo billboard merely another entrance into it? And if Peerless was actually attempting to render the domain more accessible, why safeguard it with an invitation-only gate, like some underground rave club? Unless Peerless hoped that by appealing to the cyberjock community's penchant for anything conspiratorial, stealthy, and cutting edge they could keep out the casual fliers, and commandeer only the best.

Or did the relocation of the domain have something to do with the Netquake Tech had inadvertently triggered, and its resultant effects on the Peerless Castle? Had Tech—and, by extension, Harwood—been indirectly responsible for the domain's ending up here, at the western terminus of the Escarpment?

Marz had programmed the Mace with the location coordinates of Mach Two's construct, a colossal edifice with a tapering crown, rendered all the more fortresslike by its encasing data girders and construction scaffolds. Cyber-traffic was light—only a few boxy maintenance craft flitting about—and the Mace advanced without encountering resistance.

He brought the Mace to a halt above the crown, which jutted out from the scaffolding like a perversion of Lady Liberty's torch. When Harwood had tried to enter one of the constructs in Peerless' sub-basement, Scaumlike programs had poured out in defense, ultimately chasing Harwood and Tech from the domain. Tech wondered if he would receive a similar reception. But Cyrus' existence was at stake, and chances had to be taken.

Enabling Skeleton Key—the piece of Mach Two soft that had gotten Harwood and Tech into Peerless' domain in the first place—Tech deftly unlocked a freight portal in the data scaffolding, and maneuvered the Mace through. No black programs rushed to intercept him. But even without Scaum's cohorts to pull in the welcome mat, the construct's shadowy interior chilled him to the bone.

In design, it might have been the EPA or any Network site that housed vast amounts of data, except that in place of well-illuminated corridors and tidy storage rooms the citadel was hollowed by tight passageways, and the stark nexus points where the passageways intersected. The confined burrows twisted past antiseptic-looking cavities, reminiscent of inorganic matter viewed through an electron microscope. But tucked neatly inside each chamber was a black program, faceted as a finely cut diamond, that seemed not so much in storage, as in stasis or *hibernation*—just waiting to be awakened and transferred to sites and cybercraft throughout the Network.

Tech gritted his teeth and moved deeper into the corridors.

His hands were white-knuckled on the joystick, and his feet tapped the control pedals erratically, causing the Mace to advance in fits and starts. Pounding in his ears, his heart sounded like it was submerged in water. Dealing with one Scaum had been terrifying enough. Now he had discovered an entire nest of them.

Finally he remembered how to breathe, and his slow exhalations calmed him.

He had come to the domain hoping to distract whomever or whatever was controlling the virus-dispensing dirigible anchored above the octagon. But he realized that he had a more terrible duty to discharge.

Tightening the fingers of his right hand on the

joystick trigger, he began to spray the citadel's occupied chambers with corrupting code. The prolonged scream that tore from his throat was almost loud enough to drown out the hideous screeches of whatever it was he was deleting.

From the confines of the transparent cylinder that had delivered him from the heights of his redoubt in the Rocky Mountains, Skander Bulkroad gazed down on the holographic reproduction of the Network, and saw that events were proceeding as planned.

He had moved the car perpendicular to the tower's vertical shaft, out over the holographic representation of Cyrus' octagon in the Wilds. The clever young cyberwizards employed by Data Discoveries had deployed an umbrella-like shield to protect the octagon from the virus spewing from Peerless' zeppelin. But Scaum's conscripted agents had made short work of the defensive hemisphere, which now resembled a decomposing mushroom cap. Soon the eight-sided construct itself would decay, and the process of uploading Cyrus bytes into the zeppelin could begin.

For ten years Bulkroad had borne the burden of Peerless' failure to thwart Cyrus' disappearance, and at long last the moment of rectification was at hand.

Cyrus would be back in captivity, and returned to the mission he had been designed originally to execute.

Bulkroad was savoring each nanosecond of success, when Scaum's harsh whisper issued from the audio beads Bulkroad wore in both ears.

"Our mastery is no longer assured."

Under the soft cap, Bulkroad's great dome of a head wrinkled in misgiving. "The umbrella?"

"The shield is of little consequence. Someone has entered the *domain*."

Bulkroad stared into empty space, then focused his gaze on the zeppelin, which all at once appeared to have been bled dry, and was beginning to deflate.

"How could they know about the domain?"

"Unknown. The intruder arrived in a domain craft—though one of ingeniously modified capability."

"Arrived at Mach Two?" Bulkroad said, in mounting incredulity.

"Arrived, and is deleting the transplanted brood."

"Who," Bulkroad started to say, and cut himself off. "Tech," he said through clenched teeth.

"I am diverting my forces accordingly," Scaum murmured. "This time I will deal with him."

The Mace's weapons drained, Tech began to search for a way out. He knew he was deep inside the citadel, but he didn't know how deep, or even from what direction he had come.

In his cybercidal rage—the product of a temper he had never been able to control—he had managed to lose his bearings.

He took it for granted that Peerless was aware of what he had done, and had already sent forces to deal with him. He also took it for granted that sustaining a delete inside Mach Two would be a great deal worse than being blinded by amplified code or left comatose as a result of plunging into the abyss. He contemplated performing a graceless exit from the domain, but couldn't summon the nerve.

If only Mach Two felt more like a virtual construct than a *real* one, he thought.

But there was no telling what repercussions might ensue from a graceless exit executed here.

His anxiety increased as he swerved the Mace through the citadel's bewildering maze. It was as if he were trapped in the convoluted circuitry of some gargantuan machine. Worse, every change in vector, every hairpin turn seemed to deposit him back in the same place. Time and again, even when he clung to an undeviating course, he found himself back where he started.

He called up Skeleton Key and studied the semblance of map that resolved in his visor window. The map resembled a complex mandala. But the route out seemed simple enough, so why couldn't he find it?

Blanking his mind to everything but the displayed map, he negotiated a series of twists and turns and discovered to his relief that he had somehow managed to escape the reiterating loop of confined corridors and sheathed cavities, many of them horridly defiled by the steady stream of corrupting code he had poured into them.

Then, abruptly, an anomaly appeared.

It was nothing more than a dark distension in the distance; a slight protuberance in a passageway wall that sometimes marked the opening to an exit shaft. What mattered was that the node was different than anything he had seen thus far, so he accelerated for it, flat out.

He arrived at the node sooner than he expected, and kept right on going, relieved to see its iris open at his swift approach.

But he had scarcely crossed the threshold when it shut tight, trapping him inside.

In the Data Discoveries flight room, Felix listened with limited comprehension to Marz and Isis' simultaneous attempts to bring him up to date on everything that had happened since the *Cyberchallenge* launch party at Lot 49.

In the jumble of words that streamed from the two teens—Isis in the new flight chair, and Marz at the cybersystem controls—Felix caught just enough to grasp that Harwood Strange had been returned to consciousness; that Tech's abductors were members of Strange's former posse of outlaw hackers; and that the craft of certain *Cyberchallenge* contestants were being used by Peerless in an attack against Cyrus.

When Felix couldn't take another moment of it he held up his hands for quiet, silencing Marz and Isis in midsentence.

"This was supposed to be a simple security job!" he said.

"So, like, we're fired?" Isis asked.

"Oh, and another thing," Marz said in a babble of words. "We think we found a second door into the Peerless domain on the western fringe of the grid."

Felix rolled his eyes. "Area X, Marz?"

"Yes!"

"And don't forget to tell him about Alladin," Isis added from the flight chair.

"Alladin?" Felix made the mistake of asking.

Marz nodded his head repeatedly. "A cyber-flying dog."

Felix opened his mouth to say something, but thought better of it. He turned to the dentist's chair, in which Tech was reclined, his data visor in Network-active mode and his hands clamped tightly on the joystick. "Before you confuse me with anything else, where's Tech now?"

"In the domain," Marz said. "That's what we've been trying to tell you!"

"Doing what?"

"Attacking the Mach Two construct that's controlling the dirigible."

"Oh, is that all?" Felix said, scarcely believing his ears.

"And getting results, by the look of things." Isis gestured broadly, the way people did when they were in the Network and figured naturally that everyone could see what they were seeing. "The dirigible's collapsing, and the craft that were chipping away at the octagon are leaving."

Felix and Marz glanced worriedly at each other.

"They're calling off the attack on Cyrus to go after Tech," Marz said.

Felix went to the dentist's chair and bent down over Tech to monitor his breathing. When he swung from the chair his expression was grave; his eyes narrowed. He motioned to the couch, which sometimes served as a third Network interface.

"Marz, get me a headset and joystick."

Isis raised her eyebrows at Marz. "Now we're really in trouble."

So dense was the darkness, it had texture.

Tech didn't know if he was moving or motionless, right side up or upside down, conscious or unconscious, dead or alive.

Scaum's voice resounded from every direction.

*"An upgrade is available for your craft—your flesh-and-blood craft, that is. Do you wish to upgrade now or later?"*

Cold invaded Tech's body, making him queasy and doom-stricken. A suffocating tightness gripped his chest and sent his heart galloping. In paralyzing isolation, he waited for Scaum to parade through his mind the horrors the dark entity had unleashed on the occasion of their previous encounter. He waited, too, for his memories to be riffled like a deck of playing cards, empowering Scaum to select remembrances at will, and deploy them against Tech to undermine his defenses. At that previous meeting, Tech had escaped by carrying out the equivalent of a control-alt-delete, but that wasn't an option this go-round, because he couldn't feel his hands or feet.

He was simply a mind, swimming in unfathomable darkness.

*"You've been a transcendent nuisance,"* Scaum went on. *"First by facilitating Cyrus' reassembly, then by bridging the abyss and touching off a Netquake that forced us to relocate our operations. The fall into the abyss you engineered for me was most unpleasant. I hope you don't mind my repaying you in kind."*

Hellish images began to blaze through Tech's mind, like the protoplasmic shapes and shifting colors that sometimes swam behind his eyelids after a deep-immersion Network session. Scaum sent him glimpses of a horrid landscape, a sky shot through with forking lightning, tens of thousands of tormented minds . . .

"Is this your world?"

*"The world to which my lineage was condemned."*

"Your *cyberspace*," Tech said.

Scaum made an appreciative sound.

*"You're smart, Tech. Not like the fools at Peerless who call themselves technopaths . . . But your intelligence comes as no surprise, since I know something of your past. In fact, I know a good deal about you—more, I would venture to say, than you know about yourself."*

"So, enlighten me."

"*You would first have to accept the upgrade.*"

"What do you want from us?"

"*We have searched long and hard for a species that cultivated a cyberspace suitable to us.*"

"Is that why you're commandeering cyber-craft?"

"*Craft, Tech? We're commandeering pilots.*"

Realization dawned like a remembered night-mare, and dread overcame him.

"Is, is that what you did with Harwood?"

"*Harwood is a different case. He's nearby if you wish to speak with him.*"

Before Tech could respond, he heard Harwood's voice, as if from a great distance.

"Is that you, Tech? Can you reach me?"

"Harwood!" Tech yelled—or thought he did.

"Tech! Tech?—"

"*That's enough,*" Scaum said. "*But I hope that lays to rest your concerns that he is piloting a craft for us. Think of him as . . . in storage.*"

"That's what'll happen to me? I'll become a ghost program?"

"*No. You, I will nurture like a pearl, encasing you in layer upon layer of code until you grow lustrous with data. Then I will wear you as a medal.*"

Scaum sent him visions of the process, but Tech fought down his fear.

"You're trying to trick me like the last time—when I *defeated* you."

"*Don't confuse this moment with our previous meeting, for I am long beyond tricking you.*

*Submit to me and I will tell you the truth about yourself—and about Cyrus. Cyrus knows what I'm talking about, Tech. That's why we need him returned to us."*

"I'd rather be a ghost."

*"Then you shall. But before you join Harwood, I have need of some information you possess. Cyrus will soon be ours. Which leaves only the flight plan for bridging the abyss. The Wilds were promised to us, and we shall have them."*

The dull ache Tech felt deep in his head began to expand and intensify, culminating in excruciating pain. It was as if Scaum had plunged clawed hands into Tech's brain and was tearing it open. Tech tried to build a shield around his thoughts, similar to the armor scales Marz had raised around Cyrus' octagon. But Scaum seared through Tech's defenses like a laser, turning his mind white hot.

*"If you won't surrender the flight plan, I'll be forced to wrench it from Strange,"* Scaum said. *"He's frail, Tech. He could die in the process, and you'll be responsible."*

Once again Scaum sent images to back up his words—harrowing scenes of Harwood writhing in pain, the life draining out of him . . .

Uninvited, a vivid memory surfaced of the chase that had ended in Tech's jump from the Escarpment, and Scaum's plunge into the abyss. Tech hadn't memorized the elaborate code sequences that translated as a flight plan. But Scaum was apparently convinced that if he burrowed deep enough into Tech's mind, he would uncover the mimetic imprinting of those sequences—the entire program.

Tech's mouth hung open in a silent scream that seemed to last an eternity.

Then Tech felt the link break.

The blackness that had become his entire world was pierced by brilliant shafts of amber light, and Tech suddenly found himself outside the Mach Two citadel and back in the domain, though upside down.

"Tech!" two voices yelled as he was righting his craft.

He ordered the headset visor to go wide-angle, and saw, off to his left, a hybrid cybercraft streak into view—a new-generation *tandem,* resembling two interlocked Chinese throwing stars. Tech's identification displays told him that Isis and Felix were piloting the things.

"Is that who we think it is?" Felix asked over the audio net.

A window popped open in Tech's visor showing him what Felix and Isis were looking at, and in what direction Tech should aim his scanners. Far west of the citadel he saw a malevolent smudge, a suggestion of a head—triangular and elongated—and what might have been wings or tatters of black cloth in angry motion.

*Scaum!*

It was if someone or something had catapulted him to the edge of Area X.

"How did you—"

"Pure firepower," Isis said, anticipating Tech's question.

Tech gazed at the tandem craft in wonder. "From just you two?"

"We donated some disabling code to the cause," another familiar voice said.

A group of noisy and garish craft appeared from behind the data scaffolds of the citadel, exhibiting a hodgepodge of old- and new-generation attachments that included everything from exhaust pipes, roll bars, and fins to cudgels and battleaxes.

One of the craft displayed an icon of a yapping mutt.

"Mackey," Tech shouted. "Alladin."

"We woulda come sooner, kid, but we didn't know the way in. All credit to your brother for showing us the route and modifying our ships."

Alladin's chariot-like craft came alongside Tech's and remained there. A series of urgent barks issued through his headphones.

"Tech," Isis interrupted. "Scaum's headed this way—with reinforcements."

Tech and Alladin looked to the west. The tentacled inkblot that was Scaum was hurtling back toward the Mach Two construct, with his squadron of commandeered cybernauts and craft flying tight support.

Wingmen Bios7 and Ramlock led the left-hand flank.

"We won't stand a chance against them," Tech said. "Not code to code."

"Not here, maybe," Mackey said, "but we might be able to even up the odds by taking 'em into the Wilds."

"We get them to chase us, then we rig the exit," Tech said excitedly.

"Uh, Tech," Felix said. "In case you haven't noticed, getting them to chase us isn't going to be a problem."

"What kind of phony exit do you have in mind?" Mackey said.

Tech snorted. "Not a phony one. I'm thinking of a real exit, with a surprise ending."

"A trap door kind of thing," Mackey said.

"Exactly. But we'll have only minutes to make it happen once we leave the domain." Taking a last look at Scaum, he muttered, "You want the flight plan, come and get it."

With Alladin's chariot mirroring the Mace's every move, Tech threw the modified cybercraft into a rapid bank and shot for the portal hidden in the billboard. Felix, Isis, Mackey, and the others trailed behind him, releasing what remained of their data bombs against the Mach Two fortress as they rocketed away.

Infuriated at having been hurled halfway across the domain by Tech's ragtag band of allies, Scaum defragged himself and gathered his conscripts. Their quarries were already speeding for the domain gate, either in retreat or in the mistaken belief that they would fare better in an engagement in the Network. But it made no difference. They couldn't possibly exit cyberspace in time—not without risking their sanity. Nor could they hope to triumph in contest.

They would all be his—new additions to the

commandeered force—or partners in storage with Harwood Strange.

Ordering his minions to form up around him, Scaum stretched out his wings and flew forward in pursuit. From their center he would be better able to supervise them, and guard against any inadvertent deletion of Tech's neural data. He had threatened Tech that he would pry the flight plan from Harwood Strange's mind, but in fact he was certain that the old man would die before surrendering the code sequences.

Tech and his rescuers passed through the portal well ahead of Scaum's squadron, certainly headed for the Wilds. It was just as the first few conscripts were through the gate that a violent quake began to rock the domain.

The sky began to fall, and an undulating wave of destruction rolled across the virtual landscape. To all sides, constructs began to tremble and crumble, many of them disappearing entirely, as if erased by the keystrokes of a master hand.

At the same time, Scaum heard a chorus of wrathful cries resound from the far side of the gate.

He gave thought to the possibility that Tech had set up some sort of ambush. But an ambush wouldn't account for the quake that was quickly reducing the domain to data rubble.

Then it dawned on him—even as the rest of his conscripts were vanishing through the gate and adding their vengeful howls to the chorus.

*Tech and his allies had relocated the Escarpment!*

It was Scaum's final thought as he shot through the portal and saw the abyss yawn beneath him.

## Chapter 14

**WEB WARRIORS**

Mackey's downtown loft was shuttered against the outside world—blinds drawn tightly over windows and skylights and fixtures at their lowest rheostat settings. The shave-skulled and tattooed Net outlaw and his cadre of cyberwizards sat in a loose semicircle, leaning forward on the crates and boxes that were their seats, listening intently to Felix's assessment of their situation.

"Some prospective clients have asked why we closed down our construct in the Wilds," Felix was saying. "I've been telling everyone that the octagon was irreparably damaged during the Netquake."

"Could the construct have been repaired, anyway?" Mackey asked.

Felix's shoulders heaved in a gesture of uncertainty. "Maybe with Cyrus' help. But that would only have left him further exposed."

The focal point of the hackers' semicircle, Felix sat in a tattered armchair, with Marz to one side of him, straddling a folding chair, and Isis to the other, perched on an overstuffed ottoman. Unable to keep still, and with Alladin tracking his every step, Tech paced behind them, hands thrust deeply into the pockets of his jeans and the hood of his red sweatshirt raised.

Three days had passed since Peerless' attack on the octagon, and Tech's counterattack on Scaum's now-sealed domain. Felix had reopened the Data Discoveries office to business only the previous day.

"How's Cyrus' defragging coming along?" Mackey asked.

"Slowly," Marz said. "We had to compress twelve towers of data into the four that survived the virus. I'm not sure what that will do to his bytes. As of this morning he was running at about two-thirds speed, and with a lot of glitches."

Mackey frowned. "Maybe that's for the best. Was Cyrus okay about you're coming here without him?"

"He wouldn't have it any other way," Marz said.

Halting briefly, Tech glanced at his brother and explained. "Cyrus is frightened."

"I can understand that," Mackey said. "But he can't hide in his machines forever. Peerless is going to come after him."

"Then Peerless'll have to deal with us," Tech said angrily.

Mackey smiled tolerantly. "They've already done that, Tech."

"Might've helped if Tech has told us about the warning Peerless sent him," Isis muttered.

Tech started to reply but Felix cut him off. "What matters is what we do from here on in."

"About what?" Naif asked. "We don't even know who or what we're up against—unless we're actually going to take Tech's word for what Scaum told him."

Tech whirled on him. "I don't care if you believe me or not, Naif. Scaum's species is set on taking over the Network."

"Scaum's species," the big-bellied hacker said in ridicule. "It's a program, Tech. A sophisticated one, I'll grant you, but a program—a *Peerless* program—nevertheless. For all you know, Scaum is an AI Peerless created and programmed to *believe* it's an alien."

"An AI that can seize a cyberflier's mind?" Tech said. "An AI that can implant programs into people? I don't think so."

Naif smiled tolerantly. "Mysterious lights in the sky, kid. Top-secret military craft and ball lightning become UFOs for people desperate to believe in extraterrestrials."

Tech glowered at him. "You think I *want* to believe there's some *entity* prowling cyberspace that can land fliers in a coma?"

"I have a question for you, Naif," Felix said.

"How do you explain the fact that Tech and Marz's friend Travis, along with three other *Cyberchallenge* contestants—all of them disqualified for unsportsmanlike behavior—are still in the hospital?"

Naif shrugged. "CiscoSoft claims there was a problem with the neural net interface. It jolted a couple of the contestants, so CiscoSoft voluntarily suspended the game."

"You guys, of all people, should know better than to trust what you get from the media," Felix said. "Or even from your friends in the cyberbiz. Network Security *forced* CiscoSoft to shut down the game. They know that Travis and the others are suffering from something a lot more serious than a neural net jolt or deep-immersion syndrome."

"Tech, what about the other one you knew?" Mackey asked. "The one piloting the shape-shifter?"

"Bios7," Tech said. "He could be in a coma, too. The problem is, we don't know who he is in the real world."

"Or she," Isis said.

"How much of this did you tell the CiscoSoft producer?" Chrome asked Felix.

"I didn't say anything about the domain," he said. "And I couldn't think of any sane way to inform him that his neural net might be jammed with cyberaliens."

"Bad for business, huh?" Naif said.

"Speaking of business," Felix said, smiling. "CiscoSoft's neural net is shut down, but Marz knows of a dozen others that are still hosting Peerless' spy programs, and they're going to need Data Discoveries' help in exorcising them. Before too long, we'll be a Network legend."

Chrome frowned at him. "Don't help them. Let it all come tumbling down. That way we can rebuild the Network from scratch, and make it the free realm it was meant to be."

"Chrome's right," Mackey said. "Let Network Security carry the ball for a while. This second Netquake really got their attention."

"The syscops have it backwards," Tech said. "They assume the quake was responsible for shifting the Escarpment, instead of the other way around."

Mackey laughed shortly. "The retooled Network. You know that by moving the Escarpment, we actually shifted a bunch of private havens right into the Wilds? Artist types and Starbucks'll be next."

"There goes our neighborhood," Chrome said with a sigh.

Mackey looked at Tech. "How long will the abyss hold Scaum, kid?"

Tech shook his head in ignorance. "If it counts for anything, Scaum reassembled in less than two weeks after his first plunge."

"Or was *rewritten,*" Naif amended.

Chrome acknowledged the remark with a nod. "It's ironic that, in trapping Scaum, we ended up positioning the shallow end of the abyss right behind the Peerless Castle. I'm not saying that we had any choice. But Peerless'll bridge the abyss before too long and expand into the Wilds, no matter of what we do next."

Mackey snorted. "We were going to need a new base of operations, anyway."

Naif looked at him. "Should I take that to mean you're buying into this craziness?"

Mackey glanced at Tech. "Not all of it. But we've at least gotta find out what Peerless is up to."

"We already *know*," Felix said. "Travis and Bios7 are proof that Peerless has the ability to commandeer minds. The question is, how many other minds have already been taken over?"

"I keep thinking about Mrs. Squabbish and her husband," Marz said.

"A client who came to us," Felix explained. "And she wasn't the first to claim that she knew someone who wasn't acting like him or herself."

Chrome nodded. "We've all heard the stories. But even that's been blamed on spending too much time virtual, not on things—entities in cyberspace infiltrating minds."

"Maybe we should pay Ken Squabbish a visit," Felix said. "According to his wife, Ken had been spending a lot of time in Area X before he started to change."

Isis looked at Felix and laughed shortly. "Mr. Believer, all of a sudden?"

Naif laughed in derision. "Make sure you check the back of Ken Squabbish's neck for strange lumps or scars. Telltale extraterrestrial stuff."

Isis saw Marz rubbing the back of his head distractedly and sucked in her breath. "Marz, you said the back of your head felt kind of numb after you'd been in the domain."

Marz realized suddenly that he was rubbing his head and stopped. "Yeah, but I feel fine now."

"But how do you *know* you're fine?" Isis said. "Maybe Ken Squabbish felt fine, too." Wide-eyed, she glanced around the loft. "I mean, all of us have been in the domain. How do we know that we're not carrying any—" She swallowed hard and found her voice. "—*attachments*."

Brief glances were exchanged, then everyone laughed nervously.

"Come on," Mackey said, "we're all right."

"Yeah, until one of us starts acting weird," Chrome said.

Naif grinned broadly. "As if weird has any meaning here. Like Mackey believing in cyber-aliens."

The room fell silent for a long moment, then Mackey said, "Who woulda predicted that Mystery Notes would be the one to turn Cyrus in."

"It wasn't Harwood," Tech said. "It was who-ever was using Harwood using his *body*."

"Yet another somebody who isn't acting like himself," Naif said.

"Tech or Harwood?" Chrome asked jokingly.

"I'm telling you, I heard Harwood *speak*. Scaum told me that he had put Harwood's mind in storage."

Naif nodded dramatically. "Sure he did."

"Can you be absolutely sure about anything you experienced, Tech?" Chrome asked.

Tech frowned angrily and averted his gaze.

"Listen up," Mackey interrupted. "I don't mean that it was actually Mystery Notes. But it's obvious that Peerless used him to give up Cyrus' contact codes."

"Has there been any sign of Harwood since?" Chrome asked.

Tech shook his head sadly. "Not of Harwood or Matterling. They never returned to Shady Grove."

Alladin barked urgently in reinforcement, and Chrome laughed.

"Man, that dog loves you," she said.

Tech ran his hand down Alladin's back.

Mackey nodded. "Why don't you keep 'im, Tech."

Tech glanced at Alladin, who was sitting on his haunches, panting and staring at Tech. "I can't have a dog."

"Sure you can," Chrome suggested.

"Sure we can," Isis said, stretching her hand out.

"Sure we can," Marz added, placing his hand on top of Isis'.

Tech placed his hand atop theirs.

"But you're going to pick up after him," Isis said to Tech.

Alladin raised his right paw, and added it to the rest.

Tech laughed and shrugged. "Maybe he'll come in handy."

Skander Bulkroad stood on the maintenance gantry that encircled the North Tower's holographic reproduction of the Network, his stubby-fingered hands tight on the gantry's pipe railing, and his eyes—behind magnifying lenses—sweeping over the grid, in an attempt to catalogue the drastic revision his long-time foes had engineered.

Behind him he heard the hiss of a door opening in the tower's curved inner wall, then the sound of shuffling feet on the walkway's metal-grate floor.

"Look at the damage they've done," Bulkroad said without redirecting his gaze. "Nothing is where it's supposed to be."

His visitor sniffed in mockery. "Almost a week has transpired, and you're still crying over trivialities."

Bulkroad's hands tightened on the railing. "To you the changes might appear trivial. For me, it's as if someone took a knife to the Mona Lisa."

Bulkroad's visitor sniffed again. "Don't insult me. I lost twenty of my brood because of what Tech and his allies did."

Bulkroad's expression softened, but he still didn't turn from the view. "Do backup copies exist?"

"Not for the ones that went into the abyss. I myself would have been down there—again—

had I not pulled up short at the last moment. Why didn't you tell me that the Escarpment could be moved?"

Bulkroad gave his large round head a mournful shake. "Because I didn't know." He swung slowly from the railing, caught off guard by his visitor's unexpected appearance—the towering height, unkempt hair, and long white beard. "I thought you would have abandoned your . . . loaner vessel by now."

"I plan to, in short order."

Bulkroad turned back to the hologram as Scaum came alongside him. "The octagon is gone."

Scaum nodded. "Did Cyrus survive your attempts to upload him?"

"Almost certainly."

"Then what have they done with him?"

"Wisely, they have chosen to remove him from the Network. At the moment, I imagine he's a standalone AI, though still harbored in the Data Discoveries office."

"That doesn't eliminate him as a threat."

"No, but we need to be cautious until Network Security has wrapped up its investigation of last week's Netquake. I can control most of the media spin, but even my influence reaches only so far. When things have quieted down, we'll deal with Cyrus."

"And in the meantime?"

Bulkroad took a breath and exhaled slowly. "There's much to be done. With the abyss flipped, placing its shallow end close to the castle, it can now be bridged, assuring our expansion into the Wilds. Within a few months, you will be able to begin downloading thousands of your lineage into the data-storage constructs Peerless will build there. And after we've chased out the undesirables, even casual fliers will be eager to tour the Wilds; so you'll have your pick of fliers to commandeer as conscripts."

Scaum nodded noncommittally. "Go ahead and raise your constructs. I look forward to inspecting them when I return."

Bulkroad glanced up at Scaum, in his loaner body. "Return?"

"I have been recalled to the broodship to explain this unfortunate reversal. I'll be uploading myself in a matter of hours."

"I see," Bulkroad said, scarcely managing to contain his surprise. "By the time you return, we should be ready to move on to the next phase of the Project."

"If you're not ready, I will be."

"I don't under—"

"I'll be bringing some of our soldiers along. It's time to accelerate the Project." Scaum gestured to the body he was wearing. "Our soldiers don't need to rely on loaner vessels like this one to travel outside of cyberspace."

Bulkroad absorbed it. "Do you mean they can transport themselves through the Net and materialize outside of cyberspace at will?"

Scaum allowed a nod. "On the world we were forced to leave behind, many of us were accustomed to moving about like that." He studied

Bulkroad. "Or did you think that we relied on *vehicles* as you do?"

"I . . . I never thought about it."

"Evidence of your arrogance."

Bulkroad kept his expression blank. "What do you want us to do with Harwood Strange's body while you're gone?"

Scaum gazed down the length of his human guise. "I have no further use for it. It's not to my liking, in any case. Better than making use of a corpse, but still too feeble." He met Bulkroad's gaze and shrugged. "Destroy it in any fashion you wish."

Bulkroad nodded.

"One more thing," Scaum said after a moment. "Combined, Cyrus and Tech make for a dangerous adversary."

Bulkroad lifted an eyebrow. "Cyrus, assuredly. But Tech . . . Well, he's nothing more than a talented—and very lucky—boy."

Scaum forced Strange's mouth to quirk a thin smile. "Once more, your arrogance blinds you to the truth. I learned something new about Tech during my most recent perusal of his core memories." Scaum let the statement hang in the air before continuing. "He's not who you think he is."

Bulkroad's expansive forehead creased in curiosity. "What are you talking about?"

"I'll say this much: He was designed to be different."

Bulkroad shook his head. "I don't understand."

"You will."

• • •

Tech stood on the observation deck of the Empire State Building, staring down at the city below, feeling at once at the center of the world and as far removed from that center as could be imagined.

It was an unusually warm spring evening, and even one thousand feet above the streets, the air was balmy. The setting sun, red-orange and swollen, had set the sky ablaze, and tourists to both sides of Tech were attempting to capture the glory with digital cameras, some of which were wirelessly linked to the Network for real-time transmittal. In the east, Venus was up, stationary among the lights of aircraft bound for JFK and LaGuardia airports.

Tech raised his gaze to the darkening sky, then lowered it to the buildings and the grid of streets spread out below him. He might have been inside the Network, bound for the Ribbon in one of Marz's acrobatic creations. For a moment it felt as if the real and cyber worlds were blurring together, and Tech wasn't sure to which one he belonged.

The universe had shifted under his feet, and every direction felt like a path to unknown territory—to the Wilds.

The sun disappeared below the horizon, and security announced that everyone had to leave the observation deck. Sardined among tourists from all over the globe—and wondering which, if any, might not have been acting him or herself lately—Tech rode the express elevator down to the eighty-sixth floor, then transferred to a local and rode it down to the sixty-fifth.

Data Discoveries was closed. Marz, Isis, Aqua, and the rest had left earlier that day. Alladin had gone home to Brooklyn with Felix, since Fidelia Temper had nixed the idea of the Vega brothers moving a dog into their room at Safehaven.

Tech moved silently through the dimly lighted waiting and flight rooms, and key-carded himself into the office. Moving directly to Felix's desk, he activated the switch that opened the mirrored wall, and rolled Felix's swivel chair up to Cyrus' communications station.

"Good evening, Tech," Cyrus said as his gremlin came onscreen, slightly out of focus and crazed by static. The AI's voice was tinged with melancholy.

"How are you doing, Cyrus?"

"Better—though not nearly myself."

*Like me,* Tech thought. Again, he was struck by the depth of his bond with the AI.

"Cyrus, Scaum told me something." Tech took a moment to collect his thoughts, then said: "Scaum said that he knew certain things about me and about you, and he hinted that you know much more about Scaum than you realize."

The gremlin nodded. "I have long believed that to be true, Tech. But how does Scaum's statement alter our present situation?"

Tech exhaled slowly. "Somewhere inside both of us are the answers to a lot of questions. Maybe even the answers to rescuing Mystery Notes and defeating Scaum for good."

"Perhaps, Tech. But our situations are not identical. Even if you lack access to the full range of recollections, your memory is intact. By contrast, parts of my memory are missing."

"Then we'll have to start by retrieving those memories."

"I suspect that, by now, they have been deleted."

"Maybe not. Suppose Peerless wants you whole again."

"Regardless, cyberspace is too dangerous for either of us right now."

"Then we'll convince Mackey to help us."

"And what do you and I do while our friends are risking their lives for us?"

"We use the time to look into each other's thoughts. Maybe some of the memories are nested inside you—without your realizing it. Maybe you can teach me things."

"I'm not a mentor, Tech. I don't know anything about teaching."

"You only think you don't. The thing is, we have to find a way to disappear for a while."

"Disappear?" Cyrus said. "What about your schooling?"

"This is more important than school. It's more important than anything."

"You would leave Felix, Marz, and Isis?"

"Yes—for their own safety."

"Tech, I'm a standalone now. We can't communicate through the Network. And unless you plan on requisitioning a moving van, it's not going to be all that easy to relocate me."

"I have an idea."

Cyrus fell silent for a long moment, then asked, "Are you rubbing the back of your head in thought or is there some other explanation?"

Tech kept rubbing his head. "I think it's because of something Scaum left with me."

The gremlin nodded gravely. "Scaum's assignment was to prevent me from reassembling. He has had the uncanny ability of seeking me out ever since. Perhaps he left something of himself in me, as well."

Tech had considered it from the start. But hearing Cyrus admit to the possibility made it all the more real and dreadful. He looked up at the camera that was Cyrus' eye on the office.

"Let's find out."

"When do we begin?"

"Now."

If you liked *Web Warriors: Dimension X*
see how the adventure began
with this thrilling first book. . . .

# WEB WARRIORS
# Book I
# MEMORIES END

## by James Luceno

*The place: New York City.*
*The time: any day now.*

Tech and Marz are brothers, orphans, and misfits—
except on the Virtual Network, where their hacking
expertise earns them serious cash as freelance
cyber-sleuths, running down lost information and
missing persons on the Web. A mean game of
Death Run is nothing for Tech and Marz. But
almost getting killed—for real—on a routine virtual mission by a shapeless, demonic cyber-thing
raises the stakes big time. Now they're heading
into the dark and dangerous underbelly of the virtual world to do some extreme detective work—
and crack what could be the motherboard of all
mysteries. And this death run is no game.

Published by Del Rey Books.
Available wherever books are sold.

# Visit www.delreydigital.com— the portal to all the information and resources available from Del Rey Online.

- Read sample chapters of every new book, special features on selected authors and books, news and announcements, readers' reviews, browse Del Rey's complete online catalog, and more.

- Sign up for the Del Rey Internet Newsletter (DRIN), a free monthly publication e-mailed to subscribers, featuring descriptions of new and upcoming books, essays and interviews with authors and editors, announcements and news, special promotional offers, signing/convention calendar for our authors and editors, and much more.

To subscribe to the DRIN: send a blank e-mail to join-ibd-dist@list.randomhouse.com or sign up at www.delreydigital.com

The DRIN is also available at no charge for your PDA devices—go to www.randomhouse.com/partners/avantgo for more information, or visit www.avantgo.com and search for the Books@Random channel.

Questions? E-mail us at delrey@randomhouse.com

 www.delreydigital.com